"Today I still admire the work of Roy Crane." —Basil Wolverton

"A treasure. There is still no one around who draws any better."
—Charles Schulz

"Every time I thought I had come up with something that I had thought no one else had done, damn it, I'd find that Crane or Foster had *already* done it!"
—Al Williamson

"Crane to this day is an influence. He was the true comic artist. I love the way he did characters in action, running around, jumping."
—Jules Feiffer

WASH TUBBS
AND

VOLUME 8 (1933-1934)

BILL BLACKBEARD
Series Editor

© 1989 NEA
Wash Tubbs is a trademark of Newspaper Enterprise Association
A Flying Buttress Classics Library edition © 1989 NBM
ISBN 0-918348-73-0 paperback
ISBN 0-918348-74-9 hardcover
LC 87-062174
Design by Amos Paine & Bhob
Repro graphics: Tod Jorgensen, Phil Kline, Nancy Branch.
Acknowledgments: Jim Ivey, Bob Bindig, Alice Specht

Excerpt from Ron Goulart's *The Adventurous Decade* by permission.

FLYING BUTTRESS CLASSICS LIBRARY
an imprint of

NANTIER · BEALL · MINOUSTCHINE
Publishing co. new york

Ron Goulart

Lickety Whop!

Bull Dawson

REVOLUTIONS DON'T ALL start in the same way. Some of them begin quietly and unobtrusively. It's only after one of these bowls you over that you realize it had been inexorably rolling toward you for quite a while. The strip that was a major contributor both to ending the domination of the joke-a-day feature and to the explosion of adventure strips in the thirties began quietly and unobtrusively in 1924 under the title *Washington Tubbs II*. The work of a twenty-two-year-old Texas boy named Roy Crane, it took a while to get going. Crane wasn't even sure at first of what kind of strip he was doing. Once he found out for himself, there was no stopping him. He began to write and draw like nobody before. There was an ease and grace to his stuff, an admirable pace. He mixed action, humor, and romance. There were pretty girls, brawls, chases, sound effects. It was like the movies.

Roy Crane

Royston C. Crane was born in Abilene, Texas, in 1901. He grew up in Sweetwater, a small town forty miles west of Abilene. His father was an attorney, and Crane was an only child. "My son says he became interested in art largely because he was a lonesome kid," his father recalled after Crane had started doing *Wash Tubbs*. "Roy had no brothers or sisters and he had to entertain himself. His mother and I, from the time he was a very small boy, would set him on the floor with picture books and magazines, scratch tablet and pencil and go about our business. By the time he was ten he was drawing comic strips." When Crane was fourteen he signed up for C. N. Landon's mail-order cartooning course. This was to have a major influence on his life. By 1924 Landon was also art editor for the NEA syndicate. "My early investment of $25 in the Landon course paid off," says Crane. But he had several years to fill between taking the correspondence-school lessons and starting the *Tubbs* strip.

In his high school years Crane worked at odd jobs his father found for him and as a soda jerk in a Sweetwater drugstore. He kept at his drawing. "I proposed doing an illustrated diary and received 50¢ a week from my father for it." Crane's drawing was pretty scratchy at this time, his lettering bad. He had trouble drawing girls at all. "I wish I could draw 'em," he commented under one inept sketch in his pictorial diary. As Crane remembers it, many of his part-time jobs didn't last long. "When I was sixteen years old I cut short a visit to Dallas to return to Sweetwater where my father had gotten me a job jerking soda. I was fired after a week." Celebrity being what it is, and small towns being what they are, that same drugstore took out a full-page ad congratulating Crane when *Wash Tubbs* began running in the local paper in 1930.

In 1920 Crane, like a good many other cartoonists we'll be encountering, went to Chicago to study at the Academy of Fine Arts. He stayed there six months. Among his instructors was Carl Ed, who'd started *Harold Teen* for the Chicago Tribune Syndicate the year before. One of Crane's assignments was to do a comic strip. He called his *Hash & Topsy*, and it was, significantly enough, about a brash young man who was looking for quick riches. Ed gave him a grade of Excellent. After his spell in Chicago, Crane returned to Texas. He worked on a couple of newspapers, dropped out of a couple of colleges. Wanderlust hit him hard about this time. When the dean of the University of Texas ruled that "Roy Crane is not by any stretch of the imagination qualified to remain as a student," Crane took off. As Crane put it, "When the bottom of my swimming lake blew away in a cloud of dust, I caught a freighter and went to sea." A lot of dissatisfied and restless college boys have made low-budget grand tours the same way. Crane got something extra out of his wander-

ings, experiences which would later become *Wash Tubbs* and *Captain Easy*.

Crane served as a seaman on the freighter, got stranded in Antwerp when he returned late from shore leave. He caught up with his ship in Wales, just in time to ride through a storm at sea which nearly sundered the craft. When he arrived in New York City he decided to try for another newspaper job. He was hired by the *New York World*, where he did staff art and also worked as assistant to H. T. Webster. Helping out on Webster's panels may have inspired Crane to try a panel of his own. At any rate, he eventually came up with a panel entitled *Music to the Ear*, with gags built around *Ain't It a Grand and Glorious Feeling?* sort of situations. United Features signed him up. Then tried to sell the panel. Only two papers bought it, meaning Crane and the syndicate would have been splitting a total take of $2 a week. The syndicate told Crane he might be able to unload the thing on another United Press operation, NEA. And that put Crane in contact with his former mail-order mentor, C. N. Landon.

Landon wasn't interested in a panel, but he asked his former pupil to try a comic strip. So Crane did. The strip, under the title *Washington Tubbs II*, began running in the early months of 1924. It was originally intended as a gag strip with simple, if any, continuity. "The funny situations worked out by Crane," explained the promotion copy, "bring in Wash's employer, the owner of a grocery store, and Dotty Dimple of the movies, who is Wash's best girl. Of course there is a rival which leads to amusing complications." These amusing complications did not always readily occur to young Roy Crane, and he was soon unhappy with the way the strip was going. I got the impression when interviewing him that even now, a half-century later, he is still somewhat puzzled as to why Landon bought *Wash Tubbs* in the first place. NEA already had a successful funny strip with a general-store background in George Swanson's *Salesman Sam*. There was even another Wash, the Negro cook in J. R. Williams's cowboy panels. Perhaps Landon, like the old fortune-teller Wash Tubbs was soon to encounter, had the power to see into the future. Perhaps he had some premonition of what Crane would

9

The Official Custodians of the Daily Acts of Wash Tubbs, Boots and $alesman $am—and the "Romance of America" Introduced to You

By LOUIS B. SELTZER

IT ISN'T skill with the pencil and pen alone that makes a cartoonist famous.

He may possess extraordinary talent and yet, without the ideas to breathe life and vigor into his works, he must inevitably fall by the wayside of obscurity.

In other words, ideas in cartooning are almost as essential, if not quite as essential, as the ability to express them via pen and pencil and ink.

Cartoonists of unusual talent have been known to struggle along for many years before they hit upon the idea or ideas that lifted them into sudden eminence.

Wash Tubbs II.

Roy Crane

This does not mean that they did not do fine work prior to their newly acquired prestige.

Usually they have built up on real effort that has been recognized by only a few but, thru the medium of a popularly received idea, is suddenly recognized by many.

The battery of artists and cartoonists for the Newspaper Enterprise Association at W. Third street and Lakeside avenue who draw their cartoons for The Press and many other newspapers are young men who have made themselves known from one end of the country to the other by their ideas.

In Friday's issue of The Press we, you and I spent a few minutes meeting four of these cartoonists, Gene Ahern, who draws the bombastic Maj. Hoople; J. R. Williams, who draws "Out Our Way"; Merrill Blosser, who gave us "Freckles," and Dorm Smith, who is a real "idea man" and whose cartoons, therefore, have attained for him nation-wide standing.

Today we'll meet Roy Crane, who gave us Wash Tubbs II; Edgar E. Martin, creator of "Boots and Her Buddies"; George Swanson, who each day puts $alesman $am thru his rather precarious adventures and Paul Kroesen, depicter of "The Romance of America," and a young man relied upon to give you a fine account of himself in the art world in years to come.

"Boots"

Edgar Martin

Now, what sort of a man is this who fashions the life of futile little Wash Tubbs each day, Wash Tubbs who seems to be buffeted hither and thither and yon by the uncompromising cross-currents of life and who, at the present time, is isolated on an island with ye fair damsel.

The why and wherefore of Roy Crane's own life gives one a good inkling as to why adventure constantly seeps into his comic strip, "Washington Tubbs II."

Crane was born in Abilene, Tex., in 1901, moved to Sweetwater (in the same state), a short time later, and, at the proper age, started in school.

Went part way thru Simmons College, Tex., switched to the University of Texas, and then attended the Academy of Fine Arts in Chicago, and studied drawing.

Then he returned to the university for two more years. Admits he was a poor student, which is why he quit and worked at everything from driving stakes at chautauquas jerking sodas and sorting potatoes, to sailing as a seaman on an ocean-going freighter.

$alesman $am

George Swanson

Landed in Antwerp, where he overstayed his shore leave, and missed his boat. Stranded! Appealed for help at the United States Shipping Board in Antwerp and a kind-hearted employe advanced the adventurer 400 francs.

Still determined to catch his ship he crossed the channel, saw London, and headed for Cardiff, Wales, where he found his boat and job waiting for him.

The day he landed in New York a coal hatch on board the ship exploded and the ship was burned. Ten days later Crane was working in the New York World's art department.

His next move was to NEA Service, where he created the character, Washington Tubbs II.

Nope, he isn't married.

* * *

INTENSE reader interest in NEA's "Wash Tubbs" comic strip is reflected in the following letter received by Roy Crane, who draws the feature, from a California fan:

Los Angeles, Calif.

Dear Sir:

When a man causes an upheaval in another's man family relations the least the former can do is help unravel the mystery.

My family is divided into factions over a part of your drawing and I ask your help in deciding whether I am wrong or my wife is right, being on opposite sides in the matter.

The matter of such great import is as to the name of Wash Tubbs' former pal. One of us says it's Cozy, the other says it's Gozy. If you advise us perhaps we can begin living where we left off.

Seriously, we all enjoy Wash Tubbs because it is something more than the average funny. Thanks a lot.

Yours very truly,

A. B. HEILBURN.

turn the strip into over the next few years. There wasn't much to recommend *Washington Tubbs II* in its first weeks. The comedy was thin, the drawing clumsy and ill-at-ease. Even Dotty Dimple of the movies wasn't much to look at.

Fortunately Crane remained dissatisfied. The strip had started running before he'd really thought out what he was going to do with it. He didn't feel he was particularly good at thinking up jokes. "The problem was what the hell to do . . . ideas like DeBeck or *The Gumps* or what?" Working at the NEA offices in unromantic Cleveland, Roy Crane dreamed of adventures in faraway places. "I wanted to be a hell of a long way off," he told me. "About the furthest off I could think of was the South Seas." Since Crane wasn't able to go himself, he sent Wash Tubbs. He worked up to the departure gradually. Toward the end of June 1924, Wash wanders into a fortuneteller's. He wants to find out how he's going to do with Dottie. The old crone, however, has other things to tell him. ". . . I see sunken ships—troubled waters—a strange man giving you a paper he doesn't wish to part with. Beware! There is another strange man! He smells of salt and distant lands—I see a dagger and but one eye—" A few days later an odd old seaman does give Wash a paper, but it doesn't seem to mean anything. And a burly sea captain begins to watch him. His name is Caliente Tamallo, and he's a rough forerunner of that quintessential rowdy, Bull Dawson.

One of Crane's favorite books was *Treasure Island*, and this first real adventure of Wash's was inspired by it. In the middle of August Wash suddenly disappears. He shows up a week later in San Francisco, having, like Crane in his youth, ridden the rods. He's figured out that the mysterious paper is a treasure map. He writes to his boss at the general store, "Me for th' great open spaces where men are men and boys will be boys. Yours for BURIED TREASURE and lots of it." Wash joins the crew of a freighter which will take him to Australia. From there he plans to get somehow to the South Sea island he seeks. "Before him lies romance! Adventure!" announces a caption. "And possibly dissillusionment. Who knows?"

Wash is shipwrecked before he reaches Australia. He is marooned on a desert island, which turns out to be the very island he was looking for. It is populated with sarong-wearing natives—cartoony men and pretty girls. Better at drawing women now, Crane began here to clutter his strips with the cute girls that became one of his trademarks. Tamallo, the sinister sea captain, shows up on the island. Wash triumphs over him, finds the buried treasure, and returns home to "strut his stuff." This is the first of Wash's rise to great riches, each of which will always be followed by a tumble back down to rags. In the first months of 1925 Wash again courts Dottie. He also gets fleeced by a bogus count with a money machine. The count is

the first in a long line of swindlers and con men who will take advantage of Wash. Crane, and his successor, Leslie Turner, were extremely fond of pretenders, imposters, and bunco artists.

The Wash Tubbs who begins to emerge in the strips is very much a 1920s hero. The sort of character, for instance, that Harold Lloyd had been developing in his comedy films since the early twenties, the "eager and bumbling young man" who is determined to succeed. The go-getter. He may be either timid or brash, but he is always likable. Wash Tubbs was certainly a go-getter, an optimist who believed in his own inevitable success. Crane often showed him, in the strip's first months, loafing around the grocery store studying a book titled *How to Get Rich*. Although Wash has moments when he feels "it's always me that's th' goat," he is also certain that "if I just had a chance I know I'd amount to something some day!" Crane knew what he was doing now. He abandoned the gags and the grocery store to concentrate on adventure.

Over the next two years Wash got involved in both foreign and domestic adventure. He acquired a new girlfriend, a brunette named Roxie, and got himself a sidekick. In the fall of 1926 Wash is marooned again, which leads to his meeting Gozy Gallup. Gozy is a slick, mustached young man who shares Wash's interest in action, get-rich-quick ideas, and dimpled girls. But he's not much better in a fight than the not quite five-foot-tall Wash. Teaming up with Gozy, Wash rambles round the world. They court a set of twins in Wash's

Roy Crane with liontamer Ione, the model for Tango

hometown, work at a girls' school, and then join a circus wherein Wash falls under the spell of a tough lady tiger-tamer named Tango. Crane, who had himself briefly joined a traveling circus during his college-year wanderings, continued to be fascinated with the aggressive tomboy type of girl he first used in this sequence. He never grew tired of tigers either, introducing them frequently over the years and in some unlikely places.

After their circus stint Wash and Gozy tangle with bandits in Mexico and then, while on another island treasure hunt, they meet Bull Dawson. Dawson, the thick-necked and lowbrowed sea captain, is the prince of rotten guys. He is vicious, brutal, cunning, and hypocritical. He swaggers, scowls, smashes. He picks on people smaller than himself, especially Wash, and when he punches them a BAM! sound is heard. To the rowdy Dawson everybody is a softie. He is boastful, too. While successfully beating up both Gozy and Wash, he says, "Ain't never seen the day I couldn't handle the likes o' you pretties by the boatload an' call it fun." He urges his villainous crew to action with cries such as, "Man the boat, me bully boys!" Though Wash and Gozy win out in their 1928 encounter, it is obvious that Bull Dawson is going to return someday. He's going to beat up Wash again, too, unless someone a lot tougher than Gozy takes his side. Someone, say, like Captain Easy.

It was the resolution of a desert sequence in the fall of 1928 which led to the creation of Easy. Wash and Gozy go up against the sinister Hudson Bey in order to save Princess Jada. When the two men are lost in the vast Sahara, a black harem slave named Bola finds them. Later Bola helps them overcome Hudson Bey. Then, when Wash and Gozy fall into the hands of Sheik Bumfellah, it is Bola once more who rides off to return with a whole flock of French colonial troops. Crane explained to me that his brother-in-law had kidded him about this particular sequence. "He told me you shouldn't have a eunuch save them," Crane recalled. "What you need is a two-fisted guy." He had been thinking about the character of Wash Tubbs for some time. Crane felt Wash was an underdog, somewhat like Jim Hawkins in *Treasure Island*, who "obviously had a hell of a time taking care of himself." He had these things in mind when his brother-in-law made his criticism. A few months later Crane introduced Easy to the strip. When I mentioned that the Easy of those days looked something like Tom Mix and asked Crane if he'd had the cowboy star in mind, he replied, "No . . . since this brother-in-law of mine had suggested it, I used him as a model." Easy is not a Texan like Crane, but "a Southern gentleman." He almost didn't get named Easy. "I was thinking of a name for him while walking from the studio up to get a streetcar," Crane said. "And I thought of his name, but I didn't have anything to write it down with." By the time he got around to writing the name down, Crane wasn't sure he remembered it correctly. He put down Easy, but now "I believe it was Early." Easy or Early, the captain was about to run away with the *Wash Tubbs* strip.

BULL DAWSON

In December of 1928 Wash journeyed to the tiny kingdom of Kandelabra. What with one thing and another ("He finds that Jada, a girl he once befriended in the Sahara, is in reality a princess and rightful heiress to the throne. The Grand Vizer of Kandelabra is a crook. Not only that, but he hopes to make himself king by marrying Jada and deposing goofy King Goober"), by the spring of 1929 Wash is locked up in the dungeon of an ancient fortress known as the Black Castle. "Tubbs evidently left to die," Crane tells his readers in the headline style he then was using on captions. "Ingenious device fires pistol at him as he opens door. Fears other three doors are deadly traps also." Eventually Wash does get out of his cell, but he can't find his way out of the haunted castle. "Wash wanders thru castle . . . Seeks way out after numerous close calls." Then, on the fateful day of May 6, 1929, while revolution rages outside, Wash comes upon yet another oaken door. He commences tugging on it. A hook-nosed, unshaven man looks out through the barred window in the door.

"What in blazes you up to—trying to get in here?" he snarls. "Dang foolishness, says I. I been trying to get out for months." It is Easy, and from now on, though he and Crane don't suspect it yet, Wash is going to be second banana.

Wash locates a crowbar and gets to work on the imprisoned Easy's door, asking, "American, aren't you?" "Well, yes and no," Easy replies. "Started out that way. Hang my hat on any old flagpole now. Like a flea, I reckon—most any old dog looks like home-sweet-home to me." Borrowing the crowbar, Easy breaks down the door himself. As he dusts his hands off, Wash says, "My name's Wash Tubbs—G. Washington Tubbs. Wot's yours?" "Easy. Just call me Easy." He leads Wash to a secret exit he knows about. "Er—wot'd you say your last name was?" Easy answers, "Don't recollect, suh, as I mentioned my last name." "Wow!" thinks Wash. "A hard-boiled bozo!"

The two new acquaintances have to fight their way out of the dungeon. "Down goes the navy as Admiral Tubbs is overcome by

avalanche of blows, but 'Easy' proves to be master brawler and whips three with ease." Noticing Tubbs's plight, Easy remarks, "Blazes! Looks like my runt pardner isn't doing so well." With a smashing punch he takes care of Wash's antagonist. After the brawl Wash is enthusiastic. "Oboy! Wotta scrapper! Why, you're the best I ever saw." Easy says, "Lucky I'm good then. You're terrible. Thought you said you could fight! Blazes! You couldn't lick a postage stamp. That little runt hit you so many times he . . . Why, what's the matter? Hurt your feelings, didn't I? Aw, kid, I'm sorry . . . you're O.K., son—a game kid. Bum fighter maybe, but dead game." It is the beginning of a nearly half-century friendship.

Easy, it turns out, has also been working for Jada. He's been posing as a captain of artillery, and the princess is the first one in the strip to call him Captain Easy. Actually, Easy has been serving as chief of the Kandelabran Intelligence Service. "Well, dern my sox!" exclaims Wash when he hears this. "So you're a detective!" After ending the country's civil war and putting Jada on the throne, Wash and Easy refuse high positions in her kingdom and slip quietly out of the country. After a few days in Paris the new team catches "the first boat for the USA." Back in his hometown, with Easy as his guest, Wash gets embroiled with a phony countess and finally comes to be the prime suspect in a murder case. Easy, using both his detective abilities and his fists, sets out to clear his friend. At one point the police detective, suspicious of Easy, asks him, "What's your full name? Where's your home?" "Known gen'rally as just Easy, suh. Captain Easy," he answers. "Hum! Your occupation?" "Beach-comber, boxer, cook, aviator, seaman, explorer, and soldier of artillery, infantry and cavalry, suh."

Bull Dawson, supposedly living an honest life in Wash's very hometown, recurs in the strip now. Just before Christmas of 1929, Easy and Dawson tangle for the first time. Easy suspects Dawson is mixed up in the murder, and while watching his hideout he's

Editors Requested This!
A SPECIAL INTRODUCTORY STRIP

INTRODUCING WASH TUBBS   By Crane

"WASH TUBBS" has taken the country by storm. It has forged its way to the very top. People have been talking about it everywhere.

That is why a number of editors, who are not now using this great adventure strip, have written NEA and asked that we give them a special introductory strip so that they may start "WASH TUBBS" and get their share of the circulation benefit out of the strip's popularity.

The recent murder mystery in "WASH TUBBS" had everybody intensely interested—guessing—and following the strip every day. The murder yarn is over—but the finish of it only paved the way for another great story.

When "WASH TUBBS" swings into an adventure, the story is so closely connected and so amazingly interesting and exciting, it is difficult to break in and start the strip right in the middle of the yarn.

Don't wait until this new adventure is well under way. Start with the introductory strip on this page, which is for release Tuesday, March 18—and then swing right into the regular release Wednesday, March 19.

BOTH old and new papers will be interested in a few hints as to what is to happen in the new adventure.

The introductory strip locates "WASH TUBBS" and his pal, Easy, as castaways on a deserted island. This leads to their meeting a beautiful girl and into an amazing adventure in Asia's quaintest kingdom.

There will be a dramatic war on elephants, a phantom king who cannot be killed, a villainous rajah, battles, mutiny, treachery and firing squads.

We would rather not tell you more, because you're going to get a thrill out of it yourself. We can promise, however, that the story will have action constantly—love, mystery, and a rip-snorting, surprising finish.

Ask any editor who is running "WASH TUBBS" what the reader reaction has been. Then you will want to start this adventure strip on Tuesday, March 18.

There are three promotion ads on this page for new papers, and two for all papers using "WASH TUBBS" at the time the ads release.

For release Saturday, March 15, only in papers starting "Wash Tubbs" Tuesday, March 18.

EDITORS—THESE THREE ADS ARE FOR YOUR USE IF YOU ARE NOT NOW USING "WASH TUBBS."

For release Tuesday, March 18, only in papers starting "Wash Tubbs" on that date.

For release Thursday, March 20, in all papers using "Wash Tubbs" at that time.

WORLD'S GREATEST ADVENTURER!

Everybody in (Name City) will enjoy meeting Wash Tubbs, the world's greatest adventurer.

He is coming here on Tuesday, March 18, and will remain with us from then on, as the hero of a wow adventure strip called "WASH TUBBS."

Wash is just an ordinary sort of a kid, but filled with the urge to go places, do things and see all there is to see. No part of the world is too far off for him to hie to, as long as there is adventure to be found there.

In fact, in his first appearance, March 18, he is shown as a castaway on a deserted island—with plenty of thrills ahead of him.

Watch for our new adventure strip—

"WASH TUBBS"

For release Monday, March 17, only in papers starting "Wash Tubbs" Tuesday, March 18.

CASTAWAYS ON A DESERTED ISLAND!

"WASH TUBBS," the greatest of all adventure strips, starts in the (Name Paper) on Tuesday, March 18.

The hero of this strip—WASH TUBBS HIMSELF—is a castaway on a deserted island, far out in the Pacific. He is miles and miles from everybody—except his good pal, Easy.

Easy usually can get Wash out of trouble—but this time—well, what can you do when you're a castaway?

That's what you will find out by following the thrilling daily doings in "WASH TUBBS." Start reading it—

TUESDAY, MARCH 18

PLENTY OF THRILLS IN THE OFFING

"WASH TUBBS," the greatest of all adventure strips, starts today.

Turn to Page 00 and your interest immediately will be aroused!

Wash Tubbs himself, after whom the strip is named, is a castaway on a deserted island, far out in the Pacific. His good pal, Easy, is with him.

Plenty of thrilling things can happen in a situation such as this—and PLENTY of them DO!

If you like to read things that grow and grow and grow—in interest, thrills and mystery—start, today, reading—

"WASH TUBBS"

For release Saturday, March 22, in all papers using "Wash Tubbs" at that time.

SPRING FEVER??

Betcha you feel like going places and seeing things!

But, maybe you can't do it right now.

Well, the next best thing is to travel along with "WASH TUBBS" by reading of his adventures every night in the (Name Paper).

He's the champ at going places — seeing things — and running into thrillers.

Turn to Page 00. You'll enjoy the greatest of all adventure strips—

"WASH TUBBS"

FOOD!

YOU'D be thrilled, too—if you were on a deserted island—and found a bag of meal.

"Wash Tubbs" and his pal, Easy, run into a bit of luck today—for a change.

But they still are in a pretty precarious predicament.

You will be interested every day, if you read this greatest of all adventure strips—

"WASH TUBBS"

 NEA Service, Inc., 1200 West Third Street, Cleveland, Ohio

The World's Greatest Newspaper Feature Service—Backed by 37 Years' Experience.

CLEVELAND, MARCH 10, 1930

(Printed in the U. S. A.)

---

jumped by the big rowdy. Fighting foul, as usual, Dawson whacks Easy over the head with a board, telling him, "Ain't never seen the day I couldn't whip the likes o' you in carload lots." When Easy returns home and Wash asks what happened, he answers, "Got heck beat out of me. Dawson caught me." "I betcha old Bull don't look like any chorus boy hisself." "All he got was some skinned knuckles, that's what." "Well, did you find out anything . . . ?" "All I found out, laddie, is that Bull Dawson is one tough baby." Already Captain Easy is somewhat more complex a character than the average two-fisted hero of pulps and silent movies. He doesn't always win. Nor is he always right. It turns out both he and the police are wrong about the murder. The deathbed confession of the spurious countess is what finally gets Wash off free.

Easy and Wash stick together for all of 1930 and part of 1931, getting dumped on an island by Bull Dawson, outwitting headhunters, becoming mixed up in a revolution in the Central American country of Costa Grande. In this latter sequence the team makes one of their earliest mutual quick climbs to fabulous wealth. They help an eccentric scientist sell a bomb-exploding device to the ruling party. "The Americans become the richest men in Central America. The invention is SOLD! One hundred and fifty million dollars is there!" Crane, characteristically, has the money paid to them in small bills stuffed in huge sacks with dollar signs emblazoned on the sides. And, also characteristically, the invention proves to be a fake and the money counterfeit.

In the summer of 1931 Crane decided to tell something about Easy's past. He revealed that Captain Easy's real name was William Lee. Easy was a West Point man and had been married. Now there

Frank Battle, a rarely seen Crane Sunday page, virtually unknown among Crane collectors. It was submitted to NEA in 1930, and an attached note indicates a second episode may exist.

appears, at least to Wash, to be a possibility of Easy's clearing his name and remarrying ex-wife Louise. So Wash writes his partner a note and takes off alone. "Well old pal, by the time you get this I guess I'll be on my way.... I never expected to see you marry some bon bon. I always thought you would get shot. Well I never guessed that your dad ever ran for the U.S.A. senate either—I always thought you were a bum like me because you never comb your hair I guess. Do not try to find me, I am doing what is best for your own good as I would only get you in scrapes again. Best wishes, your old pal, Washington Tubbs." Apparently Crane later wished he had kept Easy a man of mystery. "Crane said afterwards he was sorry he had revealed this about Easy," reports an NEA contemporary, "but he did it in a moment of weakness. However, Easy extracted a promise from Wash never to bring up the subject again and it was never mentioned in the strip since."

Tubbs travels away from Easy by way of freight train and truck tailgate. He has a few solo adventures, then teams up with a ski-nosed tough guy named Rip O'Day, who looks something like Buz Sawyer's Roscoe Sweeney will look. O'Day is more a sidekick type. He's not a hero, certainly not another Easy. The public, Roy Crane himself, and, more importantly, several newspaper editors around the country missed the hook-nosed captain. Easy returns in the spring of 1932, wearing a mask and calling himself the Asiatic Monster. He and O'Day get into a fight, which stretches over several

WORLD'S GREATEST ADVENTURER!

IF YOU feel like going places and seeing things but just can't do it right now—

The next best thing is to travel along with "WASH TUBBS," the world's greatest adventurer.

And this is going to be easy to do.

Starting next Tuesday "WASH TUBBS" will make his daily appearance in The Star as the star character in an adventure comic strip that is named after him.

"WASH TUBBS" is the absolute leader of all adventure strips. It's the first and last word in thrill, romance, fight, mystery, suspense and excitement!

Watch for "WASH TUBBS" on Tuesday.

---

days' strips. Easy wins, and Wash's eyes light up. "There never was but one fella could fight like him—an' 'at's old EASY. C'mon, I know you!" O'Day fades from the strip, and Easy and Wash become partners for good. Later that year, after escaping from a prison island, they get involved in another revolution. "Ex-convicts leap from hoosegow to army commands! Become big shots overnight! Pockets are lined with gold, and fame and fortune beckon." This rags to riches to rags to riches formula, frequently unfolding against a mythical light-opera-kingdom background, continued through the early and middle 1930s. "I loved those little countries," Crane told me. The war, however, was coming closer, and everything, even comic strips, was going to change.

Before we follow the Tubbs and Easy team into the real war, we'll back up in time a few years to take a look at Crane's Sunday pages. The *Wash Tubbs* Sunday began in 1929 and was, befittingly enough, small. It occupied one-third of a page above the two-thirds devoted to J. R. Williams's *Out Our Way* characters. Really this was little more than a four-color daily, with no continuity and a gag payoff each week. NEA had been talking with Crane for some time about doing a Sunday page of some sort. Early thinking had favored a completely different feature, and Crane had worked up at least two sample ideas, getting an okay for a full page that would deal with the Revolutionary War. The Crash of '29 postponed the debut of that one indefinitely. By 1933, when a full-page Sunday was again feasible, there was no doubt as to what it would be about—"We'd

THE VENTURA COUNTY STAR

The Ventura County Star

And The Ventura Daily Post, Established 1883

allowed Easy to run away with the strip"—and *Captain Easy, Soldier of Fortune* was brought forth. Easy was the absolute star of the Sundays; Wash wasn't even allowed in them for several years. The opening sequence found Easy soldiering as a pilot in the Chinese air corps. He next crossed swords with a tyranical Eastern mogul (finding time while a captive of the mogul to wrestle with a tiger, and tie a knot in its tail), outwitted a gang of Chinese pirates, hunted for treasure in a sunken city, and generally had a fine time. These early Sundays stimulated Crane, and he put some of his best work into them. Since nobody had to worry about chopping the pages into various sizes in those innocent, uncommercial days, Crane could do anything he wanted in his full pages. Panels could be any size, depending on the story he was telling and the design he had in mind, and could run all the way across the page or all the way down one side. He was able to stage Easy's adventures much more flamboy-

Make way for the great adventurer

WASH TUBBS

He arrived in Ventura today with a whoop and a cheer—he'll bowl you over with his thrilling escapades, in a new comic strip The Star is introducing, and you'll like him for his bravado.

Turn to the comic page—Page 9—and get your first glimpse of Wash Tubbs.

GIVE!

A civil appeal for charity is as much a challenge of patriotism as was ever a call to arms.

TUESDAY, NOVEMBER 17, 1931

antly in the Sunday format, to go in for much more in the way of backgrounds and action. Mountains, jungles, and eclectic palaces rose up, hordes of crazed warriors galloped across the scene, scores of harem girls lounged and languished. As Crane modestly puts it, "Doing the Sunday pages then was fun." It was in the Sundays, too, that he developed and expanded his use of sound effects. Huge BAMS accompanied explosions, YEOWS of pain decorated brawls, punches produced the sound LICKETY WHOP! While Easy is escaping, on elephant-back, with a rescued harem girl, the native drums begin sending signals. Quietly at first—bum bidy bum—but soon growing louder and more ominous—Diby Daby Dum! Dum! DUM! DUM!

Roy Crane was soon devoting most of his time to turning out the *Easy* Sunday. This meant taking on extra hands. The erratic quality of the 1930s dailies is due to the trying out of several assistants and ghosts, chief among them being Bela Zaboly. Crane was relatively satisfied with him, but NEA liked Zaboly's work, too, and gave him the *Major Hoople* panel when Gene Ahearn was lured away to King Features. Soon after that Crane asked his old friend Leslie Turner to help out for a while. Although fonder of the lighter kind of adventure sequences, Turner had the job of handling the increasingly serious *Wash Tubbs* dailies while Crane continued with the *Captain Easy* Sundays. The Sunday sequences became more and more screwball toward the end of the thirties (it was in a weekend story that Crane introduced the magical animal known as a swink). "When the war came along we switched to pretty serious stories," Crane recalls. "And that demanded serious drawing." Except on Sunday.

Leslie Turner has described his life and career this way. "When Crane left in 1943 I inherited the strip.... This chore has left little time for anything eventful." He'd been Crane's assistant and frequent ghost for several years before the strip officially passed into his hands. "In 1937 I pinch-hit for Roy Crane on *Wash Tubbs* while he frolicked in Europe," he explains. "Stayed on as assistant till he left for greener pastures." Crane had apparently thought Turner would come along to those greener King Features pastures with him. "I left NEA to do *Buz Sawyer*... expecting Les to go with me. But NEA grabbed him," Crane says. "And there I was... new strip, daily and Sunday, middle of the war, and absolutely nobody available who could give me any real help." Crane's switch to King came as pretty much of a surprise to Leslie Turner. He told me he hadn't given much consideration to carrying on *Wash Tubbs* on his own, but when the offer to take over came from NEA he accepted without hesitation. The friendship between the two men, which dates back further than that of Easy and Tubbs, survived that wartime strain. Crane eventually found not one new assistant, but several. Turner stuck with Easy for another quarter-century, quitting late in 1969, a few weeks before his seventieth

Maybe you've noticed Wash Tubbs, in the midst of some absorbing effort, with tongue protruding as he struggles. Here the cameraman caugh Wash Tubbs' pen-papa, Artist Roy Crane, doing the same thing. Then at right, Crane is seen as he looks when the drawing's all complete. Fellow artists accuse Crane of getting his characters' facial expressions by looking in a mirror.

birthday. He passed the strip, which had been called *Captain Easy* both daily and Sunday since 1949, over to his assistant.

Turner was born in Cisco, Texas, "in time to see the last week of the nineteenth century." He grew up in Wichita Falls, almost completed four years at Southern Methodist University, spent part of a term at the Chicago Academy of Fine Arts. It was in Chicago at the academy that Turner first met his fellow Texan Roy Crane. Like Crane he suffered from wanderlust in his youth and devoted his summers to riding the rods. This fondness for trains stayed with Turner and, even though he no longer traveled under them, he often built Tubbs and Easy adventures around trains. His first professional job after drifting out of college was in a Dallas engraving plant. At the same time he was sending cartoons in to *Judge*, and selling a few. After marrying in 1923, he and his new wife headed East. In New York Turner abandoned cartooning for illustration. He became a friend and protégé of the then prominent illustrator Henry Raleigh, and began doing work for *Redbook, Ladies' Home Journal*, and the *Saturday Evening Post*. Most of his illustrations were in a sober, realistic style with no trace of the lickety-whop! approach. Of course at this point, in the late 1920s, Turner had no idea he would someday be drawing a newspaper strip. What he was thinking about doing then was raising sheep. Since this was a short while before the stock market collapse, Turner perhaps sensed the need of a more dependable, down-to-earth job. He and his wife and daughters moved to Colorado. He stuck that out for three years, "drawing with one hand while rearing a herd of ungrateful sheep with the other." Finally, after another and less successful bout of freelancing in New York, Turner got the invitation from his longtime friend to come out to Cleveland and help out on *Wash Tubbs*.

"We each had our specialties," says Crane about the period when Turner assisted him. "I did the writing, drew all of the Sunday, all water and action on the daily, while he drew girls, aircraft, etc. The strip sprang back to life." At first Turner couldn't get the hang of his friend's style. He told me the most difficult thing was learning to draw with a pen again after years of using a brush. He gradually simplified his work, but for some time the energy and suppleness of the Crane approach eluded him. Turner did the daily while it was undergoing its transition from Ruritanian continuities to those involving more and more of what was going on in the real world. Easy went to work for the FBI, then got into the service. He quickly became a real captain, to avoid confusion. Wash, who'd married in the late 1930s, was less frequently seen. He stayed on the homefront working for his father-in-law, the grouchy tycoon J. P. McKee. Leslie Turner patiently rendered all the uniforms, gear, and weaponry required. What he really wanted to do, though, was comedy, and as soon as the

Second World War ended he converted to a different kind of adventure.

Although Leslie Turner most often appears as a footnote to Crane in histories of the comics, he is really a very effective artist in his own right. By 1946 he had developed a strong style, built on some of the Roy Crane foundation blocks yet individual. He is the only artist to take over a major strip and equal, and sometimes surpass, his predecessor. Crane always worked fast; Turner derived much of his drawing enjoyment from a slower and more careful approach. An excellent figure and action man, he is equally good at backgrounds. His continuities are among the most convincingly placed in comics. He can convey the look and feel of any location—a rundown English pub, a bleak stretch of southwestern desert, a brooding Victorian mansion. Turner also has a great eye for clutter, particularly lower-class clutter, which he details with as much loving care as George Price. Many of the foreign locales used in *Captain Easy* Turner didn't see first hand until after he retired, and for these he relied on scrap. For adventures unfolding in the United States he usually traveled to the spots he wanted to use. Turner enjoys traveling around the country by car, has often turned out his strips in hotel and motel rooms.

To match the new style of the postwar years, Turner came up with new characters and new kinds of continuity. For about the first year and a half of his tenure as artist, the scripts were written in NEA's Cleveland offices. Then Turner was allowed to do his own stories. From the Crane stock company he retained such as McKee, Bull Dawson, and Lulu Belle Suggs, "circus strong woman, wrestler, female boxing champ, holder of the world record in pig-lifting." He added several recurrent characters of his own, notably the Kallikak family. The Kallikaks are a vast and worthless clan of lowlifes, headed by Orville Kallikak and his wife and their nitwit son Buster. They have relatives everywhere in the world, anywhere that they might

cause McKee, Wash, and Easy new trouble. Their name comes out of psychologist Henry Goddard's studies in heredity. His Kallikak family had two branches, one good and thriving, and the other composed of criminals, idiots, invalids, and paupers. Turner's Kallikaks all belong to this latter branch. When I talked to Turner recently he said the disreputable Kallikaks were among his favorite characters. Another favorite is Buckingham Ish, the prince of swindlers. Ish has only one mark: the bald, crotchety J. P. McKee. Like all successful con men, Ish always takes advantage of his victim's desire to make a quick buck by seemingly taking advantage of someone else. It is McKee's failing that he is always ready for one more get-rich-quick scheme, and never recognizes Ish in his latest disguise. The Ish type of clever scoundrel was one of the staples of popular fiction when Turner was growing up. He says remembrances of O. Henry's Gentle Grafter gave him the idea for the audacious Ish. From the late forties onward there were many episodes using the Kallikaks and Ish, plus satires on Hollywood, advertising, and contemporary life in general. Turner

Crane inked by Turner

mixed these with straighter continuities about treasure-hunting and spy-catching. He now and then tried a serious continuity, such as one dealing with alcoholism. On this one he had a feeling the syndicate might balk, so he sat on the drawings until it was too late to do anything else and then sent them in.

For nearly a decade Turner was only responsible for the daily. When Crane left NEA in 1943 they put the *Captain Easy* in the hands of Walt Scott. So unimaginative was Scott, then nearly fifty, that he'd spent most of his life until that time in Ohio, over twenty years of it working as a newspaper staff artist in Cleveland. Though Scott later showed a modest affinity for cute whimsy in a page called *The Little People*, he was completely unsuited to doing a Crane-style adventure strip. They let him stumble along with the *Easy* Sunday, though, until the summer of 1952. Then Turner took over. He was reluctant to add the page to his chores, but it meant more money and his wife persuaded him to try it. It says something for the vitality of Captain Easy that even nine long years of Walt Scott could not destroy him. The first Leslie Turner page appeared on August 31, 1952, in the middle of a Scott story. He began signing it two months later. The extra burden of a Sunday page apparently buoyed Turner up, at least initially, and the first two years contain some of his finest work. Turner exuberantly filled the page with sweeping desert scenes, idyllic shots of the New England seacoast, panoramas of English country estates and stately homes. It abounded with vintage automobiles, ocean liners, jets, and, of course, trains. Significantly, it was a little over six months after he added the Sunday to his work load that Turner did a weekend continuity with Wag Patakey, the deadline-missing cartoonist.

Patakey, who is a composite of Turner and Crane in looks, draws the famed strip *Giddy McWaddle*. When Easy first encounters him, through his lovely blonde daughter, the cartoonist is holed up in a deserted pueblo in a southwestern Indian village. Much the same as Turner, Patakey likes to travel around the country and is continually having to stop to bat out strips to meet the syndicate deadlines.

Crane inked by Turner

Once he gets at the drawing board nothing can budge him until he is caught up. At the moment, the valley where he is working is about to be flooded by the opening of a new dam. As the water starts to rise, his daughter pleads, "We *must* get out of here before the new dam has this pueblo under water! For once you've *got* to miss a deadline!" "Never!" replies the weary-eyed cartoonist. "Move the car to the high ground and get a boat, or learn to swim . . . so you can get out to mail for me!" While Patakey slouches at his board, complaining, "I'm out of ideas! Six strips and a Sunday page every week for twenty-five years! Shakespeare didn't turn out that much!" The water continues to rise, and various vexations of a cartoonist's life are visited on him. The writer he's hired is no good; the syndicate doesn't believe his excuse for being late; the engravers are going to have two days off and the syndicate asks him to get even further ahead; a doting mother, traveling by rowboat, brings her son over for advice, saying, "He's awfully talented. . . . There ain't a billboard in the county he hasn't put a moustache on, Mr. Pattycake! An' any kind of *work* makes him sick! So if you'll show him how to be a cartoonist . . ." Finally, when the water is up to Patakey's waist, Easy carries him off and finds a way to help him get his drawings in on time. The cartoonist and his daughter invite Easy to stick around, but he replies, "Not *me!* Your racket is too nerve-wracking! I'll got dig up a bloodcurdling adventure, and relax!"

Turner stuck with the Sunday page for the remainder of the 1950s, alternating moderately blood-curdling adventures with broader farces starring Wash, McKee, Lulu Belle, the numerous Kallikaks, and Ish the swindler. After suffering a heart attack he had to give up the page. Mel Graff began ghosting the Sunday early in 1960, though Turner occasionally returned to do a page or two. The last of the Leslie Turner dailies ran in January of 1970; the final episode was about his old favorite, Buckingham Ish. Bill Crooks, assistant on the strip for nearly twenty-five years, assumed the drawing. Jim Lawrence, who'd scripted several humdrum strips previously, became the writer. When I talked to Leslie Turner late in 1974 he said he's been reading over a good many of his old proofs since he'd retired. The drawing, he felt, held up pretty well, but he thought the copy could have been a lot more concise.

Ron Goulart

WASH TUBBS

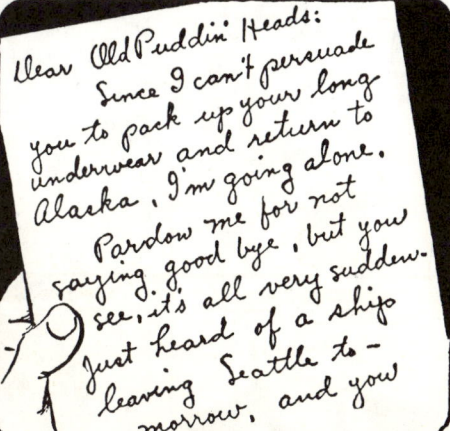

TAP TAP TAP TAP!
YOU DON'T BELIEVE IN SPOOKS? LISTEN!
FOOTSTEPS COMING DOWN THE STAIRS.
TAP TAP TAP!
THAT'S AMY— SO SAD AND LONELY— EVERY DAY SHE GOES TO THAT CHAIR AND TURNS ON THE LIGHT.
AH! DID YOU SEE IT?
CLICK!
TAP TAP TAP TAP
GOOD GOSHA MIGHTY!
SURE FUNNY! I KNOW DERN WELL THERE'S NO SUCH THINGS AS SPOOKS, YET---
OHHH, DEAR!
HEY, McQUIGGLE! COME QUICK! THEY'RE AT IT AGAIN.
VOICES! FIRST OUTA ONE WALL AN' THEN THE OTHER.
AH! THAT'S MARY, SIR. I DARE SAY YOU'LL GROW TO BE QUITE FOND OF HER, SIR. SO LOVABLE AND SAD.
OHH DEAR ME!
LISTEN! NOW THERE'S MUSIC.
HEAVENLY, ISN'T IT? MARY WAS SO MUSICAL. THIS IS HER PICTURE, SIR, BEFORE SHE WAS—AH— TAKEN AWAY. PRETTY, ISN'T SHE?
TWEET
TWEETY TEE TWEET TWEE
SHOO! THERE GOES THE TELEPHONE.
MEOW!
HA! I'LL SEE McQUIGGLE ABOUT THAT!
TWEETY TWEE TWEE

AH! A SECRET SAFE — WITH ALL TH' SPOOKY STUFF GOIN' ON AROUND HERE, I BETTER HIDE MY MONEY.
THERE! SIXTY BUCKS IN GOOD OL' GREENBACKS.
LATER:
GOT A TEN SPOT, WASH?
SURE. COME UPSTAIRS.
MY GOSH! LOOK!
IS IT GONE?
NO! IT'S BEEN CHANGED INTO SILVER.

WOTTA DAY! WOTTA HOUSE! WELL, ANYWAY, TH' SPOOKY STUFF'S QUIETED DOWN. MAYBE I CAN GET SOME SLEEP.
Wham!
Crash!
DOGGONE EVERYTHING! I GIVE UP. I'M GUNNA DRESS AND GO FOR A WALK.
REG. U. S. PAT. OFF. © 1934 BY NEA SERVICE, INC.
NOW MY CLOTHES ARE GONE!!!

LISTEN HERE, McQUIGGLE, THIS SPOOKY BUSINESS HAS GOT TO STOP. UNDERSTAND!
I'LL DO MY BEST, SIR. BUT I FEAR, SIR, THAT I HAVE VERY LITTLE INFLUENCE OVER SPIRITS.
GET THIS STRAIGHT. WE DON'T BELIEVE IN SPIRITS, AND WE DON'T INTEND TO BE SCARED OUT. WHATS MORE, WE'RE TIRED O' COOKING OUR OWN MEALS. GET SOME SERVANTS IN HERE, PRONTO.
YES, SIR.
IN FACT, SIR, I ALREADY HAVE TAKEN THE LIBERTY TO HIRE THEM.
BAH! THEY LOOK LIKE A MOB O' GANGSTERS.
YES, SIR. I QUITE AGREE. BUT UNDER THE-AH-PECULIAR CIRCUMSTANCES, SIR, IT IS IMPOSSIBLE, TO SECURE FIRST-CLASS HELP.

AFTER SPENDING A GAY EVENING IN THE CITY, WASH AND EASY MOTOR HOME.
'AT'S FUNNY. TH' PLACE IS DARK.
A HECK OF A BUTLER WE GOT! HE GOES OFF TO BED WITHOUT EVEN LEAVIN' A LIGHT.
McQUIGGLE WILL HEAR ABOUT THIS.
NOBODY ANSWERS TH' BELL, EITHER.
WHY, HELLO! THE DOOR'S OPEN.
GOSH AMIGHTY! SOMEBODY'S BIN MURDERED!
IT'S THE BUTLER!
BETTER SEE IF HE'S STILL ALIVE AND—
YEEEOWWW!
GEE WIZ! I NEVER HEARD SUCH A BLOOD-CURDLING SCREAM IN MY LIFE.
IT WAS A WOMAN. COME ON, PODNER.
EMPTY!
CAUTIOUSLY, RAPIDLY, THEY SEARCH EVERY ROOM IN THE HOUSE.
'AT'S FUNNY. THERE'S NOT A SOUL HERE.
WHAT THE BLAZES!
BOY, IT SURE IS MYSTERIOUS. SOMEBODY BUMPS TH' BUTLER OFF, A WOMAN SCREAMS FOR HELP— AN' YET WE CAN'T FIND A SOUL IN TH' HOUSE.
HUM! LET'S GET BACK TO THE BUTLER.
WE'LL HAVE TO CALL A DOCTOR FOR HIM.
AN' TH' COPS.
JUMPING BLUE BLAZES!!
HE'S GONE!
EVEN TH' BLOODSTAINS ARE GONE!
ROY CRANE

AN' HERE'S WHERE TH' BUTLER'S BODY WAS LAYIN,' OFFICER, ALL COVERED WITH BLOOD. THEN THERE WAS A WOMAN'S SCREAM, AN' WE RAN UPSTAIRS.
AND WHEN YOU GOT BACK, THE BUTLER'S BODY WAS GONE.
JUST WHERE DID THE SCREAM SEEM TO COME FROM, MR. TUBBS?
WELL, IT SEEMED LIKE IT WAS FROM RIGHT OVER-HEAD.
ABOUT WHERE THIS DOOR IS, EH?
YESSIR, BUT THERE'S NO USE LOOKIN' IN THAT ROOM, SIR. IT'S VACANT.
GREAT JEHOSEPHAT! YOU CALL THAT VACANT?
WELL, GEE WIZ! IT WAS— HALF AN HOUR AGO.
WHAT! YOU WERE IN THE HOUSE, AND YOU DON'T KNOW HOW THAT BLOOD-SWEATING HIPPOPOTAMUS GOT IN?
NOSSIR. UNLESS TH' SPOOKS BROUGHT 'IM IN.
THE SPOOKS?
YESSIR. TH' HOUSE'S FULLA THEM. VOICES COME OUTA TH' WALLS, CATS TURN INTO CANARIES, DOLLAR BILLS CHANGE TO SILVER. WHY, NOTHIN'S IMPOSSIBLE IN THIS PLACE.
BETTER QUESTION THE SERVANTS, MIKE. THESE GUYS ARE COO-COO.
I'LL SAY THEY ARE!
WE JUST TALKED TO THE SERVANTS, AND THEY SAID THE BUTLER WASN'T MURDERED AT ALL.
YEAH, THEY JUST SAW HIM. HE WAS QUITTING. SAID HE WAS FED UP ON WORKIN' FOR A COUPLA SQUIRRELS.
HE WAS AS HALE AND HEARTY AS EVER, THEY SAID.
WELL, LET'S GO HOME, BOYS. WE'RE JUST WASTING OUR TIME.
WE GOT TO FORGET THIS NONSENSE ABOUT SPOOKS, PODNER, AND HAVE A TIME. WHY, DO YOU REALIZE THAT WE HAVEN'T THROWN A SINGLE PARTY?
BUT, GEE WIZ! WE DON'T KNOW ANYBODY.
I KNOW THE BROTHER OF A MOVIE QUEEN.
A MOVIE QUEEN?
SURE! EVER HEARD OF WANDA LA DREEMA? WELL, HER NO-ACCOUNT BROTHER, OLD WINDY SMELTZENBUM, OWES ME TWO BUCKS.
YOU CAN'T GET A DATE ON THAT, Y'BIG SAP.
THE BLAZES I CAN'T! WHY, YOU DUMPY DOODLEBUG, I'LL FILL THIS ROOM WITH THE MOST GORGEOUS CREATURES YOU EVER LAID EYES ON.

SCENE: THE PALATIAL APARTMENT OF WANDA LA DREEMA, MOVIE ACTRESS.
CAP'N EASY, A FREN OF YO BROTHA, IS CALLIN', MA'M.
I NEVER HEARD OF THE BUM. IF HE'S A PAL OF WINDY'S, HE'S BROKE. TELL HIM I'M NOT IN.
DAT GEN'L'MAN AIN' BROKE, MA'M. AH SEE HIM DRIVE UP IN A TWENTY-FO'-CYLINDER PALUZA WIF TWO CHAUFFEURS.
TWO CHAUFFEURS ?
YES, MA'M. HE'S DRESS UP FIT'N TO KILL, EN SAY HE HOPE YOU'LL MOTA OUT TO HIS BIG ESTATE EN GO YACHTIN'.
YACHTING ?
YES, MA'M! HE GOT A 200-FOOT YACHT, EN HAN' ME A 10-DOLLA BILL. DAT CAP'N EASY SHO IS CLASS.
QUICK, ETHEL! SHOW HIM IN.
REG. U. S. PAT. OFF. © 1934 BY NEA SERVICE, INC.
SO CHAWMED, MY DEAH, DEAH CAPTAIN EASY. I HAVE OFTEN HEARD MY BROTHA SPEAK OF YOU.
?
WANDA LA DREEMA TRIPS IN LIKE A GA-GA ANTELOPE.
AND GUSHES NONSENSE ALL OVER THE PLACE.
SHAMEY ON YOU, FOR NOT CALLING SOONA.
YOU SEE, SINCE RETURNING FROM THE ALASKAN GOLD RUSH, WE'VE BEEN SO BUSY WITH OUR STABLE AND YACHT THAT I - - -
YOU DEAH, SWEET BOY! I'M SIMPLY WILD ABOUT YACHTS.
IT WORKED, PODNER. TWENTY MOVIE QUEENS ARE COMING OUT TO DINNER.
!
R. CRANE
REG. U. S. PAT. OFF. © 1934 BY NEA SERVICE, INC.
LISTEN, PODNER. THIS IS THE CHANCE OF A LIFETIME. IF EVER YOU ACTED CIVILIZED, DO IT TONIGHT.
I GETCHA. WE GOTTA MAKE A BIG IMPRESSION, OR WE'RE SUNK.
THAT'S THE IDEA. PUT ON YOUR BEST MANNERS, AND LAY OFF THE BONERS.
AW, LEAVE IT TO ME, EASY. I KIN BE AS SWELL A GENT AS ANYBODY.
THEN THE MOVIE QUEENS ARRIVE! 20 DAZZLING, BEAUTIFUL GIRLS ESCORTED BY A FEW MATINEE IDOLS.
THE GUESTS RAVE ABOUT THE COCKTAILS AND FOOD. CONVERSATION SPARKLES. WASH AND EASY ARE GETTING OVER GREAT, WHEN THERE'S A MOURNFUL WAIL.
YOU'RE SITTING ON MY CHEST!
!
R. CRANE

BUT, I TELL YOU, A VOICE CAME OUT OF THAT CHAIR.
DON'T BE ALARMED, PLEASE!
'AT WAS ONLY EASY, THROWIN' HIS VOICE. HE'S A VENTRILOQUIST.
WASH AND EASY MAKE A DESPERATE ATTEMPT TO SAVE THEIR PARTY.
WELL IT'S CERTAINLY NOT FUNNY-
EEK!
TURN ON THE LIGHTS!
WHAT'S THIS? ANOTHER PRACTICAL JOKE?
LAY OFF THE FUNNY STUFF, TUBBS. TURN ON THE LIGHTS.
SUDDENLY, THE "SPOOKS" GET BUSY IN EARNEST.
YA-AA-AAA
GUNNA GITCHA! GUNNA GITCHA!
HELP!
OW! SOMETHING TOUCHED ME
LIGHTS! LIGHTS! TURN ON THE LIGHTS!
POLICE!
PITCH DARKNESS! SCREAMS! PANIC! QUEER, PURPLE LIGHTS DARTING TO AND FRO. THINGS WHIZZING THRU … AIR, AND TERRIFYING VOICES COMING FROM THE WALLS AN… …EILING.... WOMEN FAINT, AND ARE TRAMPLED. AS OTHERS RUSH FOR THE DOOR.
CADS! BOUNDERS! SO THAT'S THEIR IDEA OF A PARTY.
NEVER AGAIN!
FOR TWO CENTS I'D GO BACK AND PUNCH THEIR NOSES.
BELIEVING THEMSELVES VICTIMS OF A PRACTICAL JOKE, FULLY HALF OF THE MOVIE STARS GET MAD AND LEAVE.
DESPERATELY, WASH AND EASY TRY TO SAVE WHAT'S LEFT OF THEIR PARTY.
IT WASN'T A JOKE, HONEST T'GOODNESS IT WASN'T. TH' DERN PLACE IS ALIVE WITH SPOOKS.
IT'S HAUNTED.
MERCIFUL HEAVENS!
WE'RE AWF'LY SORRY, HONEST WE ARE.
OH, WELL! LET'S FORGET IT.
WHEE! ON WITH THE PARTY. NEVERMIND THE SPOOKS.
Roy Crane
MAJESTICALLY, THE BEAUTIFUL YACHT GLIDES THRU THE WATER. GUESTS ARE DANCING ON THE AFTER DECK. ALL IS QUIET. ALL IS PEACEFUL.
THEN THE WHISTLE STARTS BLOWING.
TOOOOO!
IT BLOWS, NOT ONCE, OR TWICE, BUT DOZENS OF TIMES.
WHAT THE BLAZES YOU THINK THIS IS? A CALLIOPE?
TOO TOOOOO!
'PON MY WORD, SIR, I CAN'T FIGGER IT OUT. NOBODY'S SO MUCH AS TOUCHED THE WHISTLE CORD.
SEND FOR McQUIGGLE!
BLAST YOU, McQUIGGLE! I THOUGHT YOU SAID THERE WAS NOTHING QUEER ABOUT THIS SHIP.
TOOOOO!
YES, SIR. IT HAS ME A BIT WORRIED, SIR. I'VE NEVER KNOWN SPIRITS TO COME ABOARD, SIR, UNTIL NOW.
Roy Crane

WHO THE BLAZES IS STEERING?
BEGGIN' YER PARDON, SOR, THERE SEEMS TO BE SOMETHING WRONG WITH THE STEERING APPARATUS.
THEN HEAD FOR HOME, QUICK. THE GUESTS ARE BECOMING ALARMED.
BLAST YOU! DON'T YOU KNOW WHERE HOME IS?
SORRY, SOR. I'M GETTIN' A BIT ALARMED MYSELF, SOR. FIRST IT'S THE WHISTLE, THEN IT'S THE STEERING GEAR, AND NOW SHE'S RUNNIN' BACKWARDS. I NEVER SEE SUCH A BOAT.
THE MOVIE QUEENS ARE SCARED SILLY.
OW! HELP!!
SEND OUT AN S.O.S.
MAN THE LIFE-BOATS!
EVEN WASH AND EASY ARE BECOMING A BIT ALARMED!
MY GOSH! EVEN TH' YACHT'S HAUNTED.
SHE'S OUTA CONTROL, SIR. SHE'S DOING EVERYTHING BUT RUN SIDEWAYS.
WHERE'S McQUIGGLE?
SPEAK UP! WHERE'S McQUIGGLE?
I THINK HE'S IN THE CAPTAIN'S CABIN, SIR. BUT THE DOOR'S LOCKED, AND NOBODY ANSWERS.
COME ON, PODNER! SMASH IT! IT'S HIGH TIME WE'RE GETTING AT THE BOTTOM O' THIS NONSENSE.
WHAM!
'AT'S FUNNY. TH' CABIN'S EMPTY.
HEY! ARE YOU SURE McQUIGGLE WAS IN HERE?
YES, SIR. I'M POSITIVE.
AH HA! A SECRET CLOSET, WITH ENGINE CONTROLS, WHISTLE CONTROL, AND STEERING WHEEL. I RECKON, PODNER, THAT OUR LITTLE MYSTERY'S ABOUT SOLVED.
?
THERE! THE YACHT'S UNDER CONTROL AGAIN. BUT WHY THE BLAZES, SKIPPER, DIDN'T YOU TELL ME THIS CLOSET WAS HERE?
'PON MY WORD, SIR, I NEVER SEEN IT.
WELL, MAYBE SO, AND MAYBE NOT. ANYWAY, McQUIGGLE'S THE ONE I WANT. IF HE'S NOT THE BRAINS OF THIS SPOOK TRUST, I'LL EAT MY HAT.

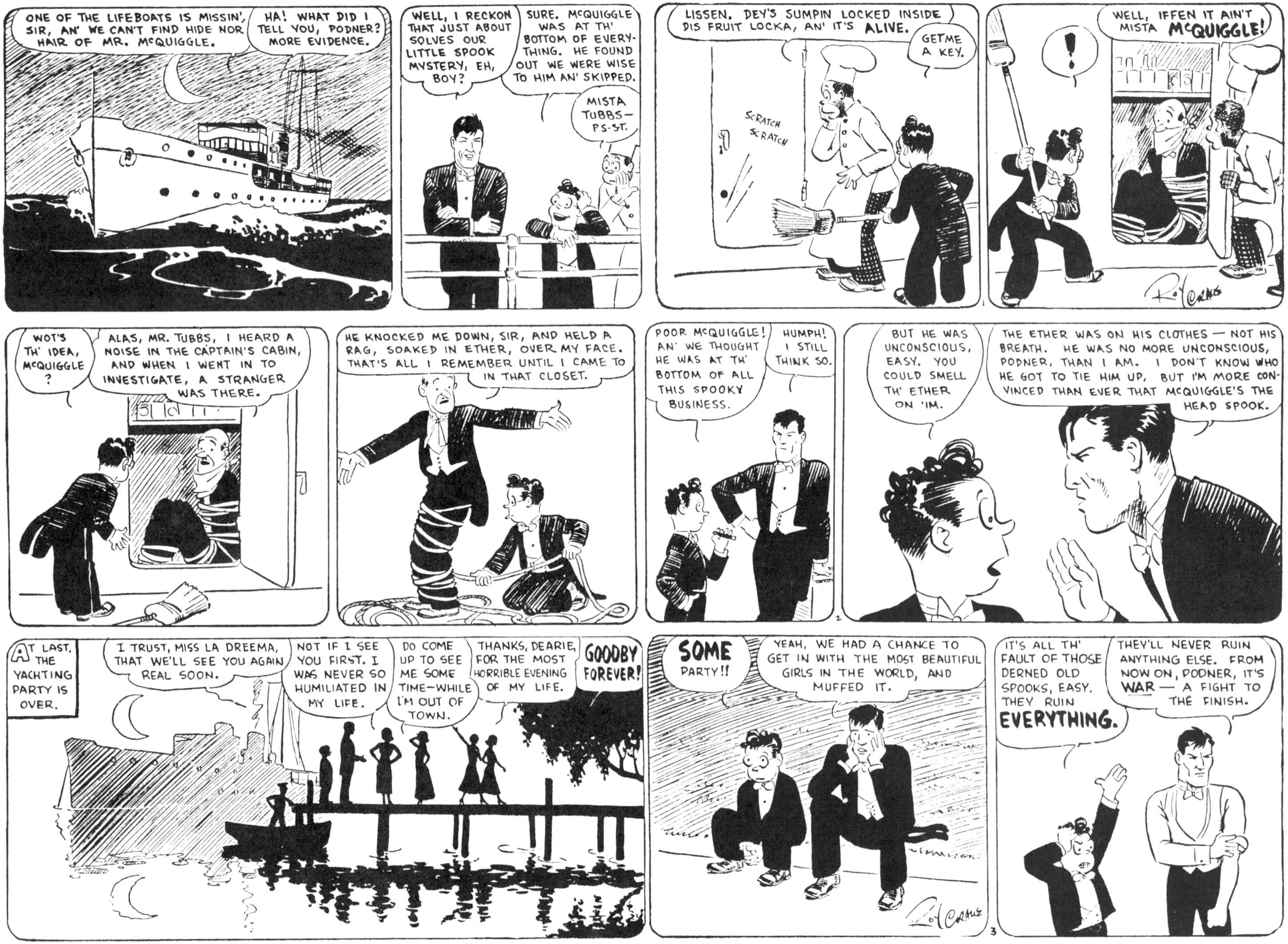

February 1934

45

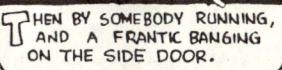

THE STRANGER IS TREMBLING. APPARENTLY IN TERROR.
DON'T LET WHO GET YOU?
THEM! THEY'RE OUTSIDE! THEY'RE AFTER ME!! THEY'LL KILL ME!
WHO ARE THEY ?
ANARCHISTS! FIENDS! ASSASSINS! FOR HEAVEN'S SAKE, PULL DOWN THE SHADES! HIDE ME!!
TAKE IT EASY, FELLA. NOBODY'S GOING TO BREAK IN.
YOU DON'T KNOW THEM! I DREW THE RED SPOT! THEY'LL STOP AT NOTHING, I TELL YOU! NOTHING!!!
ROY CRANE
SUDDENLY, EVERY LIGHT IN THE HOUSE GOES OUT. WASH AND EASY ARE STARTLED — THE STRANGER GASPS!
AH, ONLY TWO MINUTES MORE TO LIVE!
8
MYSTERIOUS STRANGER FLEES FROM ASSASSINS!
PLEADS WITH WASH AND EASY FOR PROTECTION—
THEN LIGHTS GO OUT!
9
Ka-rash!
TINKLE! TINKLE!
QUICK, PODNER! STRIKE A MATCH!
HEY! WHO'S THERE?
THERE IS THE SUDDEN CRASH OF BROKEN GLASS, AND THE STRANGER SINKS TO THE FLOOR WITH A MOAN.
BANG! BANG! POW BANG!
THEN PISTOL SHOTS! A TERRIFIED SCREAM! SCURRYING, GHOSTLY FOOTSTEPS ----- THE SMELL OF BURNT POWDER ----- THEN UTTER SILENCE.
THE LIGHTS COME ON WITH A BLINDING FLASH.
?
ROY CRANE
THE STRANGER IS GONE!!!
MORE MYSTERY!
LIGHTS GO OUT. PISTOLS BARK.
STRANGER WHO SOUGHT PROTECTION FROM ASSASSINS DISAPPEARS.
10
WITH THE HOUSE STILL HEAVY WITH POWDER SMOKE, WASH AND EASY RACE FROM ROOM TO ROOM LOOKING FOR ASSASSINS AND VICTIM.
THEY FIND NO ONE. THE DOORS AND WINDOWS ARE SECURELY LOCKED. THERE IS NO SIGN OF BULLET HOLES NOR BROKEN GLASS
10
AND McQUIGGLE STILL IS IN HIS ROOM.
WHAT HAPPENED? WHO LOCKED MY DOOR?
!
ROY CRANE

47

BANG! BANG!
HELP! MURDER!
GIMME AIR!
WHEE! GIVE 'EM TH' WORKS!
HOORAY FOR THE BRAVE FIRE LADDIES!
WHO'S THE HEAD SPOOK? STEP UP, BLAST YOU, AND TELL WHAT'S THE BIG IDEA.
HI, BOYS! MEET THE BRAINS OF THE OUTFIT?
GAIL WEBSTER!!
GAIL WEBSTER!
WHAT! YOU'RE THE HEAD SPOOK?
CERTAINLY. I'VE BEEN LIVING IN THAT ROOM FOR WEEKS.
WHAT THE BLAZES WAS THE BIG IDEA, ANYWAY?
AW, DON'T GET SORE. I CAME TO THE STATES FOR A GOOD TIME, AND I HAD IT. PLAYING SPOOK BEATS NIGHT CLUBBING ALL TO HOLLER.
YOU WERE SPENDING MONEY LIKE DRUNKEN SAILORS. IT WAS HIGH TIME FOR SOMEBODY TO PUT A LITTLE SENSE INTO YOUR EMPTY NOODLES.
JUST A MOTHER TO US, EASY.
SURE. EVERYWHERE WE GO, MAMA WATCHES AFTER US.
LISTEN, JUG-HEADS! I LIKE YOU. I'VE BEEN TRYING TO MAKE YOU SO DISGUSTED WITH THIS EASY LIFE THAT YOU'D GO BACK TO ALASKA WITH ME.
YOU DISGUSTED US, ALL RIGHT.
BUT, NIX ON ALASKA.
Y'KNOW, GAIL, WE THOUGHT ALL TH' TIME 'AT McQUIGGLE WAS AT TH' BOTTOM OF THIS SPOOK BUSINESS.
NAH, HE WAS ONLY MY ASSISTANT.
WOTTA 'BOUT TH' SERVANTS? WERE THEY IN ON IT?
SURE, I PAID THE FIRST ONES TO QUIT. THE NEW ONES WERE ACTORS, AND HAD A SWELL TIME.
GEE! IT WAS FUN, WASHIE, KIND OF A DIRTY TRICK, TOO— BUT YOU REALLY AREN'T SORE, ARE YOU?
WELL, YOU SURE RUINED US WITH TH' CLASSIEST BUNCHA MOVIE QUEENS ON TH' MAP.
SORRY, OLD POTATO. MAYBE I WAS JEALOUS. ANYWAY, I SAVED YOU MONEY. YOUR ROLL WOULDN'T HAVE LASTED THREE DAYS WITH THOSE BABIES.

WOT I WUNTA KNOW, GAIL, IS HOW YOU DID ALL THOSE SPOOKY TRICKS.
EASY, WASH. THE HOUSE IS FULL OF SECRET PASSAGES, PEEP-HOLES, AND THE LIKE. THE OWNER'S SORT OF A NUT. A PRACTICAL JOKER.
ALL I HAD TO DO WAS PUSH A BUTTON, OR YELL INTO A LOUDSPEAKER DEVICE, AND — PRESTO! THERE WERE "SPOOKS."
YEH. BUT HOW ABOUT TH' CAT TURNIN' INTO A CANARY?
EASY AS PIE. ONE CAGE HELD A CAT — ONE A CANARY. I MERELY EXCHANGED 'EM WHILE YOU WEREN'T LOOKING. I EXCHANGED THE MONEY IN THE SAFE, TOO. AND THE HIPPO, WE RENTED FROM A CIRCUS.
AN' HOW ABOUT TH' BOZO LAYIN' IN A POOLA BLOOD?
WHY, WHEN YOU RAN UPSTAIRS TO INVESTIGATE A SCREAM, HE MERELY WIPED THE CATSUP OFF THE FLOOR AND TODDLED OFF TO BED. IT'S ALL AS SIMPLE AS A, B, C.
HI HO! I'VE HAD MY FUN. I GUESS I'M READY TO GO BACK TO ALASKA, AND GET TO WORK.
WE SURE WILL MISS YOU, GAIL.
IF-IF ONLY YOU'D WAIT TILL SUMMER, WE MIGHT GO WITH YOU.
AW, IT'S NO USE. I CAN TELL. AND BESIDES, I WOULDN'T MISS THE ICE AND SNOW FOR ANYTHING.
YOU SURE BIN SWELL TO US, GAIL.
IF IT WEREN'T FOR YOU, WE'D BE FLAT BROKE.
SAY! SPREAD A COUPLE OF SMILES, YOU OLD POTATOES.
WHY, DANG YOUR HIDES! I HATE SAYING GOODBY, TOO. I LIKE YOU. BUT THERE'S NO USE GETTING WEEPY ABOUT IT. GEE WHIZ! ANYBODY'D THINK YOU WERE A COUPLE OF SISSIES.
GAIL, YOU'RE A BRICK.
EVERYBODY ASHORE WHO'S GOING ASHORE.
WELL, LITTLE PODNER, I RECKON IT'S ABOUT TIME TO SAY GOODBY.
I-I GUESS SO.

WELL, PODNER, GAIL'S GONE.
YEH. I'M READY TO GO PLACES, TOO.
WHERE'LL WE GO?
GEE! I DUNNO. SOME PLACE WITH LOTSA ROMANCE. I'M A RESTLESS ROVER, AN' I GOT GYPSY FEET. I BIN IN ONE PLACE LONG ENOUGH.
WANT ROMANCE, EH? HOW ABOUT KASHMIR, MANDALAY, MADAGASCAR, OR ZANZIBAR? OR MAYBE YOU'D LIKE PERSIA, SAMOA, TIMBUCTOO, OR RIO?
OBOY! NOW YOU'RE TALKING.
SHUX! THE MAP'S FULL O' ROMANTIC PLACES. WHY DON'T WE JUST START WESTWARD, AND—
I GOT IT! LE'S DROP A FEATHER. WHICHEVER DIRECTION THE FEATHER POINTS, 'AT'S THE WAY WE'LL GO.
READY?
LETTER DROP. WHICHEVER DIRECTION THE FEATHER POINTS, 'AT'S THE 'WAY WE'LL GO.
EAST!
SWELL! I WAS AFRAID IT'D POINT TOWARD ALASKA.
SAY, FELLA! WE FORGOT SOMETHING. HOW FAR EAST WILL WE GO? 5 MILES, OR 5,000?
GEE! I NEVER THOUGHTA THAT.
HEY! I GOT IT. LEAVE IT TO FATE AGAIN. WRITE A LOTTA NUMBERS ON SLIPS OF PAPER. THEN DRAW A NUMBER OUT OF A HAT, AN' TRAVEL 'AT MANY MILES.
O.K. BUT I HOPE IT DOESN'T LAND US IN THE MIDDLE OF THE ATLANTIC OCEAN.
HI YI! DRAW A NUMBER. WHATEVER YOU DRAW, 'AT'S TH' NUMBER OF MILES WE'LL TRAVEL.
HERE GOES!
WHAT DOES IT SAY?
400 MILES!
WHAT! ONLY 400 MILES? HECK! I THOUGHT WE'D GO WAY OFF TO SOME ROMANTIC PLACE LIKE SPAIN, OR TURKEY.
OH, WELL! HOW MUCH MONEY'LL WE TAKE? ALL OF IT?
LEAVE IT TO LADY LUCK. I'LL WRITE DIFFERENT AMOUNTS ON SLIPS OF PAPER, AND WE'LL DRAW AGAIN.

51

FOUR O'CLOCK IN THE MORNING.
HEY! WE'RE ALMOST TO PRAIRIE DOG.
A BRIEF STOP — WASH AND EASY JUMP OFF — AND THE FRIENDLY LIGHTS OF THE TRAIN DISAPPEAR IN THE DISTANCE.
HUM! NOT OVER-POPULATED, I MUST SAY.
THERE MUST BE HOUSES AROUND, SOME PLACE, EASY. I HEAR DOGS HOWLIN'.
PRAIRIE DOG
THOSE, YOU FATHEAD, ARE COYOTES.
?
ROY CRANE
REG. U. S. PAT. OFF. © 1934 BY NEA SERVICE, INC.

March 1934

COMES THE DAWN, AND THE METROPOLIS OF PRAIRIE DOG IS REVEALED IN ALL ITS SPARKLING GLORY.
JUMPING BLUE BLAZES! AND THIS IS WHERE WE CAME FOR ROMANCE AND EXCITEMENT.
WOTTA NAME
CAN'T ALWAYS GO BY A NAME, FELLA. THE PRETTIEST GIRL I EVER KNEW WAS NAMED MYRTLE BUGGELMOX.
PRAIRIE DOG
ROY CRANE
MAYBE PRAIRIE DOG HAS HIDDEN CHARMS.
YEH, I BET. AN' WOTTA WE GUNNA DO? SET AN' WAIT FOR SUMPIN TO HAPPEN? WHY THERE'S NOT EVEN A DRINKA WATER HERE.

WASH AND EASY ARE KEENLY DISAPPOINTED IN PRAIRIE DOG.
GEE WIZ! THERE'S NOT EVEN ANY WATER.
I'M AFRAID WE BETTER HOP A FREIGHT, PODNER. WE GOT TO HAVE WATER.
WOW! 60 MILES AN HOUR! I'D LIKE TO SEE ANYBODY HOP A TRAIN, AROUND HERE.
THEN WE'LL HAVE TO HIDE OUR THINGS, AND WALK.
ROY CRANE
YEH. YOU START WAITIN' FOR ROMANCE TO COME ALONG, IN THIS DUMP, AN' YOU'LL END UP A SKELETON.

BLAZES! THE FIRST DRINK O' WATER ALL DAY.
AN' TH' FIRST SHADE.
FOR HOURS WASH AND EASY PLOD ALONG THE RAILROAD TRACKS BEFORE COMING, AT LAST, TO A WATER TANK.
YOU BOYS LOOK KINDER TUCKERED OUT. BETTER COME OVER AND SET DOWN TO A PLATE OF BEANS.
OBOY! WILL WE!
SAY, FELLA, YOU'RE A FRIEND IN NEED.
WAL, Y'SEE, THIS HERE'S RANCHIN' COUNTRY. NUTHIN BUT DESERT. DON'T NOBODY EVER GIT OFF HERE, AND I GIT SORTER LONESOME.
BY THE WAY, YOU BOYS DIDN'T HAPPEN TO RUN ACROST OLD MAN RIVERS, DID YOU? HE COME BY AWHILE AGO, LOOKIN' FER SOME MEXCUNS.
WHO'S HE? THE SHERIFF?
NAW. IKE SPOTTS IS SHERIFF. OLD MAN RIVERS OWNS THE DIAMOND-BACK-T. THIS HERE'S THE NAWTH PASTURE.
OH! A RANCHER?
WAL, HE THINKS HE IS. AIN'T A BAD SORT FER AN EAST-ERNER, THO. OWNS LAND PLUMB TO THE BORDER, AND THEN SOME.
LOOKS LIKE THE OLD MAN COMIN', NOW. YOU BOYS SET STILL A MINUTE. I FIGGER HE'LL BE WANTIN' TO SEE YOU.
AIN'T BIN NO FREIGHTS BY, MR. RIVERS, BUT I PICKED UP A COUPLE OF BOYS HOOFIN' IT THRU.
THEY KNOW ANYTHING ABOUT CATTLE?
WOT CATTLE?
HUMPH! VERY EVIDENT THEY DON'T. CAN YOU RIDE? SHOOT?
OH, SURE.
WELL, MIGHT GET BY, IN A PINCH. NEED COWHANDS. RIP-SNORTERS. NEED 'EM BAD. I'LL GIVE YOU EACH A HUNDRED A MONTH, AND EXPENSES.
!
© 1934 BY NEA SERVICE, INC. REG. U. S. PAT. OFF.

100 A MONTH AN' EXPENSES, OBOY!
PSST! TOO MUCH, WASH. THERE'S A CATCH TO IT SOMEWHERE.
MAKE UP YOUR MINDS. HAVEN'T GOT ALL DAY. I'LL DOUBLE MY OFFER.
200 A MONTH! COME ON, EASY.
WAIT! THERE NEVER WAS A GREEN COWPUNCHER WORTH THAT MUCH AT HONEST WORK.
HANG YOUR IMPUDENCE, SIR! I'M A GENTLEMAN.
© 1934 BY NEA SERVICE, INC.
HONEST WORK. EASY MONEY. YOU CAN TAKE IT, OR LEAVE IT.
O.K. WE'LL TAKE IT.
I DON'T GET THE IDEA, SUH, YOU PAYING 200 A MONTH FOR COWHANDS.
THEY STRUCK OIL OVER BY EL DORADO. PAYING BIG MONEY. NOT A COWHAND LEFT ON THE PLACE.
BUT WE DON'T KNOW BEANS ABOUT CATTLE.
DOESN'T MATTER. YOU CAN RIDE, SHOOT. I'LL DRESS YOU FIT TO KILL. YOU'LL DO. YOU'LL DO.
BUT I STILL DON'T GET THE IDEA.
GUESTS COMING. FRIENDS FROM THE EAST. NEVER BEEN WEST OF PHILLY. GOT TO IMPRESS 'EM, SEE. GOT TO PUT ON A SHOW.
THIS IS MY FOREMAN, APACHE JOE, THE FAMOUS INDIAN SCOUT AND GUNMAN. HE'LL SHOW YOU THE ROPES.
?
WAL, OVA YONDA'S THE MAIN HOUSE. YOU AIN'T ALLOWED THERE NO TIME.
BACK HEAH'S THE CORRALS, BUNKHOUSE, AN' SECH. THET'S WHEAH YOU BELONG.
LINE UP WITH THE REST O' THE NEW HANDS AND GIT YORE OUTFITS.
YES, SIR.

BOY! WOTTA TOUGH LOOKIN' BOZO THAT APACHE JOE IS!
AND HE'S OUR FOREMAN, TOO.
OLD MAN RIVERS SAYS HE'S A FAMOUS GUNMAN AN' INDIAN FIGHTER.
AW, DON'T BELIEVE WHAT THE OLD MAN TELLS YOU. THAT'S OLD JOE COOLEY. HE NEVER FIT NOBODY.
NO?
NAW. HE RUNS THE HODWEAR STORE OVER IN EL DORADO. BUSINESS IS KINDER SLOW, AN' JOE'S JES HELPIN' OUT WHILE THEM GUESTS FROM THE EAST IS HEAH.
!
12

COME GIT YORE OUTFITS, BOYS. VAQUERO COSTUMES TO THE MEXKINS, CHAPS TO THE COWBOYS, 'N' SIX-GUNS ALL AROUN'.
13
OBOY!
AN' LISSEN HEAH, YOU BLINKIN' HOOT OWLS—IF I SEE ANYBODY IN OVER-ALLS AFTER THEM EASTERN GUESTS GIT HEAH, HE'S FIRED!
REG. U. S. PAT. OFF. © 1934 BY NEA SERVICE, INC.

WOT TH' HECK!
BUFFALOES. THE OLD MAN RENTED 'EM FROM A ZOO OVER IN CALIFORNIA.
14
AN' INDIANS!
SURE. HE AIN'T NO PIKER. GUNNA PAY 'EM TWO BUCKS A DAY, JUST TO SQUAT AROUND, AND FURNISH ATMOSPHERE FOR THEM EASTERN GUESTS.

EE-YAH! EVERYBUDDY OVER TO THE BUNK HOUSE FOR CHOIR PRACTICE.
CHOIR PRACTICE ?
YAS, CHOIR PRACTICE!
BUT I CAN'T SING A LICK.
NOBODY'S ASTIN' YOU TO BE NO GOL DURN CANARY.
BUT EVERY COWBOY'S GOT TO KNOW COWBOY SONGS – IT'S THE OLD MAN'S ORDERS. AN' IF'N YOU CAN'T SING A TOON, YOU KIN GARGLE IT.
© 1934 BY NEA SERVICE, INC.
REG. U. S. PAT. OFF.
ONCE AGAIN BOYS – LOUD AN' MOURNFUL.
OH, BURY ME NOT ON THE LONE PRAI-REE, WHERE THE WILD COYOTES WILL HOWL O'ER ME, IN A NARROW GRAVE JUST SIX BY THREE, OH, BURY ME NOT ON THE LONE PRAI-REEE.
NOW, THE OLD CHISHOLM TRAIL, WHOOP 'ER UP!
OH, A TEN DOLLA HOSS AND A FAWTY DOLLA SADDLE – AN I'M GOIN' TO PUNCHIN' TEXIS CATTLE – COMMA TI YI YOUPY, YOUPY YA, YOUPY YA.
THAT'S FINE! AN' THE FUST ONE O' YOU PEACOCKS I HEAH YAPPIN' SOME NEW-FANGLED FOX-TROT, I'LL TAKE A BRANDIN' IRON TO YA!
NOW, SADDLE YO' HOSSES. THE OLD MAN'S BORRIED A GENU-WINE STAGE COACH FROM A MUSEUM, AN' HIM AN' HIS EASTERN FRIENDS IS ON THE WAY.
YIP, YIP, YIPEE! WHEE!
WHEE! BANG! BANG BANG! BANG! BANG YIPEE! BANG BANG BANG! BANG!
I BET WE GAVE THOSE GUESTS THE THRILL O' THEIR LIVES, EH, PODNER?
DIDJA SEE 'EM? DIDJA SEE 'AT GOOD LOOKIN' GIRL? BOY, OBOY! WOTTA SWEET JOB THIS IS GUNNA BE!

EVERYBODY IS TALKING ABOUT THE GOOD LOOKING GIRL WHO WAS AMONG THE NEWLY-ARRIVED GUESTS.
I DIDN'T SEE NO GAL.
ME NEITHER. ALL I SEEN WAS A FAT OLD MAMA WHO LOOKED LIKE SHE'D 'SWALLERED A PICKLE.
NO, NO, SEÑOR. THAT EES NOT THE WAN. THEES WAN EES BEAUTIFUL!
MAYBE THE OLD MAN'LL WANT ONE OF US TO TAKE HER OUT AN' SHOW 'ER THE RANCH.
HOT DOG!
BUT IT'S THE MIDDLE-AGED FOREMAN, "APACHE" JOE, WHO IS SELECTED TO ESCORT THE GIRL.
LUCKY STIFF!
WHUT DOES HE KNOW ABOUT GALS?
WHY DON'T THEY GIVE SOME YOUNG GUY A BREAK?
WAL, ONE THINGS SARTIN, BOYS, SHE'LL SOON GIT TIRED O' THAT OLD FOSSIL. THEN IT'S OUR TURN.
WOT'S SHE LIKE, APACHE?
WHAT'S WHO LIKE?
THE GIRL! THE SNAPPY BON BON YOU JUST BIN RIDIN' WITH.
YOUNG MAN, I CAN'T SEE HIT'S ANY OF YORE DAD BURN BUSINESS.
AW, COME ON, APACHE, YOU AINT SWEET ON HER, ARE YOU?
SUTTINLY, NOT. I GOT A WIFE AN' FAMILY.
AND, EVEN IF I WAS, I GOT ENOUGH SENSE NOT TO GO COURTIN' NO BEAUTIFUL HEIRESS TO MILLIONS, LIKE MISS LANE—EVEN IF SHE IS LONELY.
A LONELY HEIRESS!
HOT DOG!
WHEE!
R. Y. CRANE
MISS LANE, ALONE, MEETS WITH THE APPROVAL OF THE COWBOYS.
PSST! Y'EVER NOTICED HOW SAD'N WISTFUL SHE LOOKS?
YEAH. SORTER HONGRY LIKE. I SHORE HOPE SHE AIN'T IN LOVE.
THEM? OH, THEM'S BISON.
YOU DON'T SAY? WHY, THEY LOOK JUST LIKE BUFFALO.
THE OTHER GUESTS ARE PUT DOWN AS BEING SAPS.
THEY MOSEY AROUND, RUBBERING AT EVERYTHING AND GETTING IN THE WAY.
FANCY SEEING REAL INDIANS!
OH, LOOK! HE'S SMOKING HIS PAPOOSE. OR IS IT HIS TOMAHAWK?
FUNNY! THE GIRL NEVER PALS AROUND WITH TH' OTHERS. SHE'S ALWAYS ALONE.
R. Y. CRANE

ONE O' YOU BOYS SADDLE A HOSS, AND TAKE IT UP TO THE BIG HOUSE.
TUBBS WILL. HE NEEDS THE PRACTICE.
TH' HECK I DO. SADDLE IT YOURSELF.
YOU DAD BURN IDIOTS! IT'S FER MISS LANE!
HEY! LEGGO! YOU SAID I NEEDED PRACTICE.
WAIT! YOU AIN'T EXPERIENCED. I BETTER SADDLE THET HOSS MYSELF.
NO YOU DON'T! WE'LL DRAW STRAWS.
HEY! I'M IN ON THIS.
ME, TOO!
TUBBS WINS!
BAH!
YOU LUCKY STIFF! I'LL GIVE TWO BUCKS TO TAKE YOUR PLACE.
NOT ON YOUR LIFE. OBOY! THIS IS MY LUCKY DAY.
AH, GOOD MORNIN', MISS LANE. WUNNERFUL DAY FOR A RIDE, ISN'T IT?
I HADN'T NOTICED, BUT WHY TWO HORSES?
WHY, AH- Y'SEE, I THOUGHT I BETTER GO WITH YOU — JUST IN CASE OF BANDITS, Y'KNOW.
I PREFER TO RIDE ALONE, THANK YOU.
BUT IT'S AWF'LY DANG'ROUS. HONEST! WHY, A GIRL WITH BIG, BEAUTIFUL EYES LIKE YOURS---
IF I NEED ANY HELP, SIR, I'LL DROP YOU A CARD.
© 1934 BY NEA SERVICE, INC.
HECK! THREE STRIKES, AN' OUT. I GUESS I DIDN'T MAKE MUCH OF AN IMPRESSION.
WELL, WELL, ROMEO! I SEE THAT THE CHARMING MISS LANE DIDN'T CARE FOR YOUR COMPANY.
YEH, SHE GIMME TH' HIGH HAT. TO HECK WITH 'ER!
SHE'S JUST A STUCK UP SNOB.
HUM! I WONDER.
SEE HER, UP ON THAT HILL? THEY SAY SHE RIDES UP THERE TWICE A DAY — ALL ALONE — AND JUST SITS AND LOOKS.
YEH. PROB'LY SHE GOES UP THERE SO SHE CAN STICK HER NOSE UP A LITTLE HIGHER.
THAT'S SOUR GRAPES, PODNER. MY GUESS IS THAT SHE HAS A REASON FOR WANTING TO BE ALONE.

OBOY! WOTTA NIGHT! JUST LOOKIT THAT MOON, EASY.
SH-H!
YOU HEAR THAT?
WHY, IT SOUNDS LIKE SOME-BODY CRYIN'!
LOOK! IT'S MISS LANE.
WOT TH' HECK DO YOU S'POSE IS WRONG?
PSST! COME ON. POOR KID! SHE'S BUSTED UP ABOUT SOMETHING —OR SOMEBODY. AND I RECKON IT'S NONE O' OUR BUSINESS.
I'M WORRIED, APACHE. WORRIED! THOUGHT THIS TRIP WOULD DO MY NIECE, MISS LANE, LOT OF GOOD. JUST MADE MATTERS WORSE. SHE GOES AWAY ALONE. CRIES EVERY NIGHT.
YES, SUH.
GOT TO DO SOMETHING, APACHE. GOT TO DIVERT HER MIND. NEED MORE ROMANCE.
WAL, THEY'S SOME FAIR-TO-MIDDLIN' COWHANDS AROUND, SUH, BUT I DON'T KNOW HOW THEY ARE ON ROMANCE.
ROMANCE, APACHE, NOT LOVE! ROMANCE OF THE WEST! EXCITEMENT! ACTION!
I RECKON YOU MEAN LIKE ROPIN' AN' SHOOTIN' AN' BREAKIN' BRONCS.
EXACTLY! EXACTLY! THE SOONER, THE BETTER. ANYTHING EXCITING, APACHE. ANYTHING.
TRYING TO CHEER MISS LANE, THE BOYS AT THE RANCH PUT ON A RODEO. IT'S A PRETTY GOOD ONE, TOO, AND THE GUESTS ARE DELIGHTED.
ALL BUT MISS LANE, WHO SITS OFF BY HERSELF AND HARDLY NOTICES WHAT IS GOING ON.
DANGED IF I AIN'T STUMPED, MR. RIVERS. SHE DON'T TAKE NO INTEREST IN NUTHIN, AN' GITS SADDER'N EVER.
EXACTLY. GOT TO TRY SOMETHING NEW, APACHE. SOME-THING DIFFERENT.
© 1934 BY NEA SERVICE, INC. T. M. REG. U. S. PAT. OFF.

I GIVE UP, SUH. WE PUT ON A DANG GOOD RODEO FER THAT MISS LANE, AND LOOK! SHE UPS AN' WALKS OFF WITH A SHOTGUN.
WHO'S THAT THROWING UP TIN CANS FOR HER?
POW!
COW-PUNCHER NAMED EASY.
IT'S A LOT OF FUN. WHY DON'T YOU TRY IT?
O.K. THROW UP THIS LITTLE ONE.
BANG! BANG! BANG! Bang! BANG!
HEAVENS ABOVE! WHY, YOU USED ONLY A REVOLVER, AND HIT IT EVERY TIME.
I RECKON, MAM, THAT'S BECAUSE YOU DIDN'T THROW IT VERY HIGH.
GOOD BOY! GOOD BOY! HE'S IMPRESSED HER
MISS LANE LOOKS AT EASY IN FRANK ADMIRATION.
YOU'RE MARVELOUS. WHERE DID YOU EVER LEARN TO SHOOT LIKE THAT?
OH, HERE AND THERE. CENTRAL AMERICA AND AROUND.
CENTRAL AMERICA? WHAT ON EARTH EVER TOOK YOU TO CENTRAL AMERICA?
REVOLUTIONS.
SAY! YOU INTEREST ME IMMENSELY. WHY, I THOUGHT YOU WERE JUST A PLAIN COWPUNCHER. WHAT'S YOUR NAME?
EASY.
I MEAN YOUR REAL NAME. WHO ARE YOU?
THAT, MA'M, IS AS PERSONAL A MATTER AS WHY YOU CRY EVERY NIGHT.
OH, PAR-DON ME! I HAD NO IDEA YOU WERE SO DESPERATE A CHARACTER.
!
OLD MAN RIVERS LOOKS ON IN AMAZEMENT, FOR MISS LANE IS NO LONGER SAD AND WISTFUL—SHE'S SMILING.
WHO, ME?
YES, YOU. MY BOY, YOU'VE FASCINATED MY NIECE. SHE'S NOT THE SAME PERSON.
IF YOU'LL PODDON MY SAYING SO, SUH, MISS LANE IS BORED. ALL SHE NEEDS IS EXCITEMENT.
BUT WE'VE ALREADY TRIED A RODEO.
NAH! I MEAN REAL EXCITEMENT. SHOOTING. WILD, WESTERN BLOOD AND THUNDER—MAYBE A BANDIT RAID.
A BANDIT RAID?
SURE. HIRE SOME FELLAS TO STAGE A FAKE HOLD-UP, AND THE BRAVE COWLADDIES WILL DASH UP AND SAVE THE DAY. IT'S SURE FIRE, SUH. IT CAN'T MISS.
FROM THIS MINUTE, MY BOY, YOUR PAY IS DOUBLED.
MAH

WAT! YOU WEESH ME TURN BANDIT, SEÑOR?
NOT A REAL ONE. YOU AND THE BOYS JUST PRETEND YOU'RE BANDITS.
IT'S ONLY IN FUN, SAVVY? HOLD UP MY GUESTS. GIVE 'EM A SCARE. ACT BAD. THEN THE COWBOYS ARRIVE — LOTS OF SHOOTING—AND YOU RUN.
AH, BUT I NO LIKE THE SHOOTING, AMIGO.
TUT TUT! IT'S ONLY IN FUN. HERE'S A BOX OF BLANK CARTRIDGES. USE 'EM. ABOVE ALL, USE NOTHING BUT BLANKS.
© 1934 BY NEA SERVICE, INC. T. M. REG. U. S. PAT. OFF.
HA! I ONDERSTAN'. GEEV THE GUESTS THE BEEG SCARE. MAKE THE BEEG NOISE. HA HA! EES A GOOD JOKE, NO?
THAT'S THE IDEA, PEDRO. AND HERE'S $50 ON ACCOUNT.

April 1934

HERE YOU ARE, BOYS. BLANK CARTRIDGES AL' AROUND.
OBOY! THIS IS GUNNA BE GOOD!
THEM EASTERN FOLKS'LL GIT THE THRILL OF THEIR LIVES. HAW-HAW-HAW!
THE BOYS ARE ELATED OVER THE COMING FAKE BANDIT RAID.
THIS HEAH MEXKIN YOU HIRED TO PLAY BANDIT, SUH—ARE YOU SURE YOU KIN TRUST HIM?
ABSOLUTELY, APACHE. ABSOLUTELY.
WAL, I DUNNO. THEM GUESTS HAS A LOT O' MONEY AND VALUABLES. IT'D BE A MIGHTY BIG TEMPTATION FER HIM TO DOUBLE-CROSS YOU.
POO POO! PEDRO'S HONEST AS THE DAY IS LONG. MEEK AS A LAMB. OWNS A LITTLE SHEEP RANCH. KNOWN 'IM FOR YEARS, APACHE, YEARS.
© 1934 BY NEA SERVICE, INC. T. M. REG. U. S. PAT. OFF.

WHILE THE BOYS AT THE RANCH ARE LAUGHING AT WHAT A SWELL JOKE THE FAKE BANDIT RAID WILL BE, SOME OF THOSE HARD FELLOWS OVER IN THE BAD LANDS HEAR OF IT.
YOU SAY OLD PEDRO, THE SHEEPHERDER, IS GOIN' TO HOLD UP OLD MAN RIVER'S GUESTS, AN' THE COWPUNCHERS IS TO RIDE UP, SHOOTIN' BLANKS?
YEAH. THAT'S IT.
AN' YOU SAY HIS GUESTS HAVE A LOT OF MONEY?
HOG RICH. GOT DIAMONDS BIGGER'N HOSS FLIES.
THEN, WHUT IN TARNATION'S TO KEEP US FROM BEATIN' OLD PEDRO TO THE HOLD-UP, AND GITTIN' THEM THINGS OURSELVES?
THET'S EGGZACKLY WHUT ME 'N' PANCHO WUZ THINKIN'.
MAYBE, AMIGO YOU CARE TO COME WEETH US, NO?
© 1934 BY NEA SERVICE, INC. T. M. REG. U. S. PAT. OFF.

62

BANG! BANG!
ZIP
ZIP
RUN, YOU DANG FOOL! YOU CAN'T WHUP 'EM WITH BLANKS.
FOR A MOMENT EASY STANDS HIS GROUND, DISREGARDING FLYING BULLETS.
YIPEE!
BANG! BANG!
THEN HE TURNS AND RUNS WITH THE REST. THE BANDITS, FIRE A FEW SHOTS AT HIS HEELS, AND CALMLY RIDE AWAY.
OLD MAN RIVERS GALLOPS UP, AND EVERYBODY IS YELLING AT ONCE.
PEDRO DOUBLE-CROSSED US!
HEY! YOU SAID THEY WAS GOIN' TO SHOOT BLANKS.
LOOK AT MY ARM. I'M BLEEDING.
MY WORD! MY WORD!
9
POLICE! POLICE!
OH, MY PEARLS! MY PEARLS ARE GONE!
© 1934 BY NEA SERVICE, INC. T. M. REG. U. S. PAT. OFF.
ROY CRANE
THE GUESTS ARE WEEPING AND WAILING HYSTERICALLY. OLD MAN RIVERS IS SPEECHLESS. NOBODY KNOWS EXACTLY WHAT HAPPENED.
BANDITS FLEE WITH $20,000 LOOT!
FAKE HOLD-UP, FOR AMUSEMENT OF GUESTS, GOES HAYWIRE.
COWBOYS ARE SURPRISED AT BEING GREETED BY BULLETS INSTEAD OF BLANKS.
YOU! YOU! I THOUGHT YOU WERE FINE AND BRAVE. YOU'RE YELLOW! YOU'RE ALL YELLOW! ONLY FOUR BANDITS, AND WHY DIDN'T YOU CHASE THEM? YOU RAN LIKE RABBITS!
WHY-AH-MY HOSS WAS SHOT OUT FROM UNDER ME.
THE BOYS FEEL LIKE TWO CENTS. BUT WHAT IS THERE TO SAY? HOW CAN THEY EXPLAIN?
HA! YOU WERE TOO BUSY RUNNING TO BORROW ANOTHER. THE MOST MARVELOUS SHOT ON THE RANCH, AND YOU HIT NOTHING! WHY, YOU CHEAP SHOW-OFF, I COULD PUT UP A BETTER FIGHT WITH A CAP PISTOL AND A HOBBY-HORSE.
ROY CRANE
© 1934 BY NEA SERVICE, INC. T. M. REG. U. S. PAT. OFF.
10
SUDDENLY, ALL ARE STARTLED BY A SHOUT.
BANDITS! BANDITS! COMIN' THEY'RE BACK!!
TH' BANDITS ARE COMIN' BACK!
COME ON, BOYS! LET'S GIT 'EM.
HOT DOG! NOW I GOT REAL BULLETS.
WE'LL SHOW 'EM WHO'S YELLA.
THIS TIME, HOWEVER, IT REALLY IS PEDRO AND HIS UNSUSPECTING SHEEPHERDERS. AT THE FIRST WHINE OF A BULLET THEY RUN FOR THEIR LIVES.
CARRAMBA! I SINK THEY GO LOCO.
HEY! WASS THE BEEG IDEA? DON' YOU WEESH A BANDIT RAID?
ONE'S ENOUGH, YOU LOP-EARED IDIOT! BRING BACK THAT JEWELRY.
WHY, THEM'S NOT THE SAME MEN, RIVERS.
11
YOU MEAN IT WASN'T PEDRO WHO HELD UP THE RANCH?
NO, SUH. NOT IF THAT'S PEDRO.
GOOD HEAVENS! THEN IT WAS A REAL HOLD UP.
ROY CRANE
© 1934 BY NEA SERVICE, INC. T. M. REG. U. S. PAT. OFF.

YOU AND YOUR SMART IDEAS—BAH! THANKS TO YOU, YOUNG MAN, MY GUESTS HAVE BEEN ROBBED OF $20,000. YOU HEAR THAT? TWENTY THOUSAND DOLLARS!
MISS LANE THINKS YOU'RE A COWARD, AN' TH' OLD MAN BLAMES YOU FOR THE HOLD-UP. BOY, YOU'RE 'BOUT AS POPULAR AS THE ITCH.
YOU DON'T HAVE TO RUB IT IN, YOU DUMPY DOODLE BUG. DON'T I KNOW IT?
GIVE ME THAT RIFLE, WINDY. I'M GOING AFTER THOSE BANDITS.
HEY! WAIT! I'M GOIN' WITH YOU.
12
EVEN BEFORE MR. RIVERS CAN PHONE THE SHERIFF, WASH AND EASY HAVE PICKED UP THE TRAIL AND STARTED OUT.
JUST US TWO, OLD PODNER. THAT'S THE BEST WAY.
Roy Crane
STEP ON IT, IKE. RIVERS SAID THEY WAS AHEADIN' FER BUFFALO GAP.
HALF AN HOUR AFTER WASH AND EASY START AFTER THE BANDITS, THE OTHER COWBOYS TAKE UP THE TRAIL.
AT THE SAME TIME, THE SHERIFF AND TWO DEPUTIES LEAVE TOWN, HOPING TO HEAD THE BANDITS OFF AT THE MEXICAN BORDER.
MEANWHILE, WASH AND EASY HAVE LOST THE TRAIL.
SAND! THE BLASTED WIND'S COVERED UP THEIR TRACKS
IT'S A CINCH THEY WENT UP THIS GAP.
Roy Crane
HUM! I'M NOT SO SURE, PODNER. THEY'RE NOT IN SIGHT ANY LONGER, AND THERE'S 50 CANYONS THEY MIGHT O' TURNED UP.
13
THE COWBOYS, LED BY OLD MAN RIVERS AND APACHE, MEET WASH AND EASY COMING OUT OF BUFFALO GAP.
WHUT'S THE MATTER?
LOST THE TRAIL IN THE SAND.
YOU DON'T HAVE TO FOLLOW NO TRAIL, YOU BLINKIN' COYOTES. THE BANDITS IS HEADIN' FER MEXICO, THRU THIS HEAH GAP.
THAT'S WHAT WE THOUGHT, AT FIRST. WE FIGGER, NOW, THAT THEY TURNED UP ONE O' THESE CANYONS, BUT THERE'S NO TELLING WHICH ONE.
FIDDLESTICKS! YOU COME WITH US. WE BRUNG SOME INJUNS— THEY CAN TRAIL ANYTHING.
© 1934 BY NEA SERVICE, INC. T. M. REG. U. S. PAT. OFF.
14
SEND 'EM BACK TO THE RANCH, APACHE. WON'T HAVE 'EM. THAT HOOK-NOSED IGNORAMUS HAS CAUSED ENOUGH TROUBLE
Roy Crane

BOY, 'AT'S APPRECIATION. OLD MAN RIVERS WON'T EVEN HAVE US ALONG.
NEVER MIND, FELLA. I HAVE ANOTHER PLAN.
WASH AND EASY ARE SENT BACK TO RANCH
WHERE ARE THE BANDITS, SHERIFF? DIDN'T YOU CAPTURE THEM?
WE AIN'T EVEN SEEN 'EM.
BANDITS ELUDE AMBUSH SET FOR THEM.
TOO DARK. NO SEE UM TRACKS. GIVE UP.
OH, MY WORD! MY WORD! WE CAN'T GIVE UP.
INDIANS FAIL TO FIND TRAIL.
16
WHAT A SILLY LITTLE FOOL I WAS!
COMPLICATIONS ARISE! MISS LANE, ATTEMPTING TO FOLLOW HER UNCLE, RIDES INTO DEVIL'S CANYON, AND IS LOST!
HAVING NEVER BEEN LOST BEFORE, MISS LANE DOESN'T KNOW WHAT TO DO.
I GUESS I'LL UNSADDLE MY HORSE, AND WAIT UNTIL MORNING.
OH, DEAR! IF ONLY I HAD A FIRE.
SHE'S PRETTY SCARED. COYOTES HOWL ALL NIGHT, AND ONCE SHE HEARS THE SCREAM OF A PANTHER.
MORNING COMES, AND HER HORSE IS GONE!!
17
REALLY FRIGHTENED, NOW, AND RAVENOUSLY HUNGRY, SHE BEGINS HURRYING THRU A MAZE OF STRANGE, BEWILDERING CANYONS.
HELP!
ON AND ON LITTLE MISS LANE WANDERS, BECOMING MORE HOPELESSLY LOST EVERY MINUTE.
HELP!
EET SOUN' LAK A WOMAN.
FOUR RIDERS STOP---
HAF A CARE, AMIGO. EET MAY BE A TRAP.
NAH. COME ON.
AND DEBATE WHETHER OR NOT THEY SHOULD INVESTIGATE THE CRY.
18
BUENOS DIAS, SEÑORITA.
SUDDENLY THEY BURST INTO VIEW. MISS LANE SCREAMS, FOR SHE RECOGNIZES THEM INSTANTLY, AS THE BANDITS WHO RAIDED THE RANCH.

66

67

WATCH THIS FELLA, WASH. IF HE TRIES ANY TRICKS, LET 'IM HAVE IT. I'LL ATTEND TO THE OTHERS.
I GOT 'IM.
QUICKLY, EASY SELECTS A HIDING PLACE AND WAITS FOR THE BANDITS.
STICK 'EM UP, BOYS! I GOT YOU COVERED.
STARTLED, THE BANDITS START TO OBEY------
Roy Crane
© 1934 BY NEA SERVICE, INC. T. M. REG. U. S. PAT. OFF.
26
THEN, SEEING THAT EASY IS ALONE, THEY REACH FOR THEIR GUNS.

INSTEAD OF THROWING UP THEIR HANDS, THE BANDITS REACH FOR THEIR GUNS. EASY SHOOTS!
BANG!
THE LEADER SINKS TO THE GROUND.
THAT'S THE WAY, BOYS. HOLD 'EM UP — IT'S GOOD FOR YOUR HEALTH. BRING YOUR PRISONER, PODNER. TAKE THEIR GUNS, AND BANDAGE THIS FELLA'S SHOULDER.
BY NEA SERVICE, INC. T. M. REG. U. S. PAT. OFF.
Roy Crane
27
CAPTURED!
ALONE, WASH AND EASY HAVE RECOVERED THE STOLEN JEWELRY, AND NABBED ALL FOUR BANDITS.
BOY! DO THEY FEEL PROUD!

WASH AND EASY ARE PROUDLY ESCORTING THE FOUR BANDITS DOWN THE CANYON, WHEN THEY HEAR A LOT OF SHOOTING,
GUARD THOSE MUGS, PODNER. I'M GOING TO RIDE AHEAD AND SEE WHAT IT'S ALL ABOUT.
SURE.
AND, TO EASY'S SURPRISE, HE COMES UPON OLD MAN RIVERS, APACHE JOE, THE SHERIFF, AND A DOZEN COW-BOYS AND DEPUTIES SURROUNDING AN ADOBE HUT.
28
GIT FER COVER, YOU IDIOT! YOU WANT TO GIT YORE BRAINS BLOWED OUT?
THE BANDITS IS HOLDIN' MISS LANE PRISONER.
WE GOT 'EM SURROUNDED.
BANG!
BANG!
BANG!
© 1934 BY NEA SERVICE, INC. T. M. REG. U. S. PAT. OFF.

69

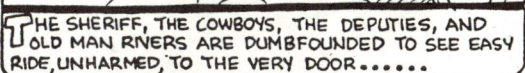

WHAT! THE BANDITS ESCAPED?
THEY GOT AWAY?
MY STARS! AND WE BIN SHOOTIN' AT NUTHIN BUT EMPTY HATS.
NATURALLY, THE DEPUTIES AND COWBOYS FEEL PRETTY CHEAP.
QUICK! WHERE'D THEY GO? WHICH WAY?
DON'T BE ALARMED, SUH.
AS YOU CAN PLAINLY SEE, MY PODNER AND I HAVE THE SITUATION WELL IN HAND.
HAYFOOT—STRAWFOOT—HEP-HEP!
MY STARS ALIVE! DID YOU BOYS CAPTURE ALL FOUR BANDITS BY YOURSELVES?
SURE! WE GOT BACK ALL TH' JEWELRY, TOO.
WELL, DANG MY. HIDE!
AND MINE, TOO.
MY WORD! MY WORD! I SIMPLY CAN'T UNDERSTAND HOW YOU DID IT.
WELL, SUH, IT SEEMS THAT MY PODNER AND I AREN'T SUCH NO-GOOD, COWARDLY, IGNORAMUSES AS SOME PEOPLE THOUGHT THAT'S HOW!
PLEASE! PLEASE! I APOLOGIZE. YOU'RE BOTH SPLENDID AND BRAVE. MY WORD! I-I----
I WANT TO APOLOGIZE, TOO. I THINK YOU'RE SIMPLY WONDERFUL, EASY. YOU'RE THE BRAVEST MAN I EVER MET.
YOU MUST JOIN US AT A TABLE OF BRIDGE.
EDGAR, RUN GET THE CAMERA. WE MUST SHOW THEIR PICTURES TO OUR FRIENDS BACK EAST.
YOU DEAR, BRAVE BOYS. YOU SIMPLY MUST TELL US AGAIN HOW YOU CAUGHT THOSE HORRID DESPERADOES.
RETURNING TO THE RANCH, WASH AND EASY ARE LIONIZED BY THE GUESTS.
THEY'D BE KISSING US NEXT.
THEY CAN'T STAND IT, THO, AND TAKE TO THE HILLS.
AH, WELL! THERE'S ONE GOOD THING ABOUT BEING HEROES, PODNER. WE'RE SITTING PRETTY WITH MISS LANE!

RETURNING FROM THE HILLS, WASH AND EASY SLICK THEMSELVES UP FIT TO KILL.
SEEN MISS LANE AROUND, APACHE?
WHY, AIN'T YOU HEARD? SHE WENT HOME YESTIDDY.
HOME?
YEAH. I RECKON IT WAS KIND OF SUDDEN. A LETTER COME FER HER, 'N' SHE GOT ALL UPSET 'N' CAUGHT TH' FUST PLANE EAST.
WELL, WHAT DO YOU KNOW ABOUT THAT?
GEE! 'AT SURE LETS TH' WIND OUTA MY SAILS. BOY, I LIKED THAT GIRL.
THE OLD MAN WANTS TO SEE YOU, EASY.
THANKS, NIFTY.
TELEGRAM FOR YOU.
YES, SUH.
ABSOLUTELY NO ONE I CAN TURN TO IN TIME OF DANGER BUT YOU STOP I IMPLORE YOU TO COME WITH UTMOST SPEED BETTY LANE
IT'S A TELEGRAM FROM MISS LANE. SHE'S IN SOME SORT O' DANGER. WANTS ME TO COME AT ONCE.
YES, YES, I KNOW. ARE YOU GOING?
WHY, I RECKON SO. IT'S SO SUDDEN, THO! I HAVEN'T HAD TIME TO THINK.
GOING TO TAKE THAT LITTLE TUBBS FELLOW ALONG?
YES, SUH. SHE DIDN'T MENTION HIM, BUT I'M SURE SHE EXPECTS HIM.
SPLENDID! SPLENDID! GET YOUR THINGS. I'VE ALREADY MADE ARRANGEMENTS FOR YOUR TICKETS. YOU'LL BARELY HAVE TIME TO CATCH THE 11:15 PLANE AT EL DORADO.

QUICK, PODNER! WE'RE CATCHING THE 11:15 PLANE AT EL DORADO.
WOTSA MATTER? DID WE GET FIRED?
ARE WE IN TROUBLE ?
NO, MISS LANE IS. WE'RE GOING EAST TO HELP HER.
WOT KINDA TROUBLE?
DANGER. GOT A TELEGRAM BEGGING US TO COME QUICK. THAT'S ALL I KNOW.
HEY, WAIT! I FORGOT MY PAY CHECK.
I HAVE IT IN MY POCKET. EVERYTHING'S TAKEN CARE OF. STEP ON IT, NIFTY!
© 1934 BY NEA SERVICE, INC. T. M. REG. U. S. PAT. OFF.

YOU DARLINGS! YOU'LL NEVER KNOW HOW RELIEVED I AM.
AFTER A FLIGHT ACROSS THE CONTINENT, WASH AND EASY ARE MET AT THE BRISTOL AIRPORT BY MISS LANE.
YOU SEE, SINCE YOU CAPTURED THOSE WESTERN OUTLAWS, I'VE HAD TREMENDOUS CONFIDENCE IN YOU.
AW, WE WERE JUST LUCKY, MISS LANE.
WELL, MAYBE YOU CAN BRING US SOME LUCK. WE NEED IT. AND, BY THE WAY, CALL ME BETTY. IF ANYBODY ASKS, YOU'RE MY COUSINS, AND YOU'RE VISITING ME.
© 1934 BY NEA SERVICE, INC. T. M. REG. U. S. PAT. OFF

NICE PLACE. WHAT DOES YOUR DAD DO, BETTY?
HE'S PRESIDENT OF A BANK, HERE IN BRISTOL.
AND WHAT'S THIS DANGER YOU SPEAK OF?
REALLY, EASY, I DON'T KNOW. IT SOUNDS SILLY, BUT I HAVE A FEELING THAT SOMETHING TERRIBLE IS ABOUT TO HAPPEN.
YOU SEE, DAD AND I LIVE HERE ALL ALONE. LATELY, HE'S BEEN TERRIBLY UPSET AND WORRIED, BUT HE WONT TELL WHAT'S THE CAUSE.
HUM! HIS BANK IN GOOD SHAPE?
SPLENDID. AT LEAST, EVERYBODY SAYS IT IS. I'M NOT SURE, BUT I THINK DAD'S BEING BLACKMAILED.
?
© 1934 BY NEA SERVICE, INC. T. M. REG. U. S. PAT. OFF

BLACKMAIL, EH?
YES, I THINK SO. ANYWAY, I'M POSITIVE DAD'S BEEN GETTING THREATENING PHONE CALLS. I LISTENED IN ON ONE.
HAS HE REPORTED THEM TO THE POLICE?
NO. HE SAYS IT'S JUST A JOKE. I'M NO CHILD, THO. I CAN SEE HOW DEATHLY PALE HE GETS.
THEN WHY DON'T YOU REPORT THEM?
I HATE TO ADMIT IT, BUT I- I'M AFRAID DAD'S IN TROUBLE—THAT HE'S DONE SOMETHING WRONG. IF I CALLED THE POLICE, I MIGHT MAKE MATTERS WORSE.
REALLY, I'VE BEEN DESPERATE FOR WEEKS. DADDY'S SUCH A PEACH. I'VE GOT TO HELP HIM. I'VE GOT TO! BUT I DON'T KNOW WHERE TO START.
YOU POOR KID!
DON'T WORRY, BETTY. WE'LL TEND TO THIS.
ROY CRANE
© 1934 BY NEA SERVICE, INC. T. M. REG. U. S. PAT. OFF.
HERE'S SOMETHING ELSE MYSTERIOUS. LAST NIGHT SOME ONE BROKE INTO THIS WALL SAFE.
ANYTHING MISSING?
NOTHING OF VALUE. YOU SEE, THIS WAS MOTHER'S ROOM. SHE KEPT HER JEWELRY IN THE SAFE, BUT SINCE HER DEATH, WE'VE SELDOM USED IT.
ANY WINDOWS OR DOORS FOUND OPEN?
THAT'S ANOTHER STRANGE THING. THERE WASN'T A CLUE AS TO HOW ANYONE GOT INTO THE HOUSE.
BY THE WAY, WHO'S THAT?
JOE, THE COOK'S HUSBAND. HE'S SORT OF A HANDY MAN. WHY?
HE'S TOO DERN SNOOPY, 'AT'S WHY!
ROY CRANE
© 1934 BY NEA SERVICE, INC. T. M. REG. U. S. PAT. OFF.
DID THE BURGLAR TAKE ANYTHING EXCEPT WHAT WAS IN THE SAFE, BETTY?
THAT'S ANOTHER STRANGE THING. NOTHING ELSE WAS TOUCHED.
WE'LL GO BACK, PODNER, AND EXAMINE THE SAFE FOR FINGER PRINTS.
HEY! WHAT THE BLINKING BLUE BLAZES?
© 1934 BY NEA SERVICE, INC. T. M. REG. U. S. PAT. OFF.
I'M SURE JOE DIDN'T MEAN ANY HARM, EASY. POOR FELLOW! HE MEANS WELL, BUT HE'S FRIGHTFULLY DUMB.
YEAH. DUMB LIKE A FOX.
WE'LL KEEP AN EYE ON THAT BIRD.

I WONDER WHERE DAD IS? HE USUALLY COMES HOME MUCH EARLIER THAN THIS.
HERE COMES SOMEBODY, NOW.
DADDY! GOOD HEAVENS! WHAT HAPPENED?
TUT TUT, BETTY. NOTHING SERIOUS, I ASSURE YOU.
SLIGHT TRAFFIC ACCIDENT AT MAIN AND FIFTH. THE CAR IN FRONT OF ME STOPPED RATHER SUDDENLY. I BUMPED INTO IT, AND HIT MY FACE ON THE STEERING WHEEL.
WHY, HOW AWFUL!
© 1934 BY NEA SERVICE, INC. T. M. REG. U. S. PAT. OFF.
ROY CRANE
YOU BELIEVE THAT YARN, PODNER?
NAH! I BETCHA SOMEBODY BEAT TH' TAR OUTA HIM.

AND WHO ARE THESE YOUNG MEN, BETTY?
THEY ARE SOME BOYS I MET OUT WEST. I ASKED THEM TO VISIT US UNTIL THOSE MYSTERIOUS PHONE CALLS STOP.
EH? WHAT'S THAT? WHAT'S THAT?
PLEASE DON'T BE ANGRY, DADDY DEAR. YOU SEE, I GET AWFULLY FRIGHTENED, HERE ALONE.
AND THEY'RE EVER SO NICE.
HUMPH! BUT KEEP 'EM OUT OF THE BANK, UNDERSTAND. I WON'T HAVE ANYBODY MESSING AROUND MY AFFAIRS.
AND FURTHERMORE, THEY'LL EAT IN THE KITCHEN WITH KATE AND JOE.
THEY'LL DO NOTHING OF THE SORT. THEY'RE MY GUESTS.
BOY! WOTTA HIT WE MADE WITH OLD DADDY DEAR.
ROY CRANE
© 1934 BY NEA SERVICE, INC. T. M. REG. U. S. PAT. OFF.

AT THE FIRST OPPORTUNITY, EASY SNEAKS OUT.
S-SST. YOU STAY WITH BETTY, PODNER. I'M GOING TO CHECK THE OLD MAN'S STORY OF THAT ACCIDENT.
HUM! JUST AS I THOUGHT.
HE FINDS MR. LANE'S CAR UNDAMAGED.
NAW, NOT T'DAY. BUT THERE WAS A PEACH DAY BEFORE YESTIDDY.
STOP
NOR CAN HE FIND ANYONE WHO SAW A COLLISION AT MAIN AND FIFTH.
SURE. ALL US KIDS SEEN 'IM, DIDN'T WE, WARTS?
I'LL SAY.
BRISTOL NATIONAL BANK
ROY CRANE
© 1934 BY NEA SERVICE, INC. T. M. REG. U. S. PAT. OFF.
FURTHERMORE, HE LEARNS THAT J. J. LANE HAD A BLACK EYE BEFORE LEAVING THE BANK.

ON THE DAY WASH AND EASY ARRIVE IN THE EAST, A CONSIGNMENT OF FLOUR IS DELIVERED TO A MID-WESTERN PENITENTIARY.
AND HUSH WATSON, WORKING IN THE PRISON BAKERY, IS DELIGHTED TO FIND THREE MARKED SACKS, EACH CONTAINING AN AUTOMATIC.
AHUK! HUK!
© 1934 BY NEA SERVICE, INC. T. M. REG. U. S. PAT OFF
TWO HOURS LATER, HE STROLLS PAST NOTORIOUS IRON-JAW LADRONI AND JOEY-THE-EEL GRUFFO. HE COUGHS TWICE SIGNIFICANTLY.
PRISON GUARDS CONTINUE THEIR MONOTONOUS VIGIL, LITTLE DREAMING THAT WITHIN A FEW HOURS ONE OF THE MOST SEN SATIONAL PRISON BREAKS IN HISTORY WILL OCCUR.
BAROOM!
A TERRIFIC AND MYSTERIOUS EXPLOSION ROCKS THE PENITENTIARY.
SIRENS SCREAM. STARTLED GUARDS HURRY FORWARD.
RATTA TA TATTA TA TAT
WAITING THUGS, OUTSIDE THE WALL, MOW THEM DOWN WITH SUB-MACHINE GUNS.
© 1934 BY NEA SERVICE, INC. T. M. REG. U. S. PAT. OFF.
THEIR AUTOMATICS BLAZING, IRON-JAW LADRONI, HUSH WATSON, AND JOEY-THE-EEL GRUFFO PLUNGE THRU THE SHATTERED WALL.....
....LEAP INTO WAITING CARS, AND DISAPPEAR.
RESULT: THREE DANGEROUS CRIMINALS AT LARGE. FOUR GUARDS DEAD, OR DYING.
EXTRA! EXTRA! IRON-JAW LADRONI ESCAPES!
ALL ABOUT THE BIG PENITENTIARY EX-PLOSION!
BUYING A PAPER, EASY RETURNS TO THE LANE MANSION.
WHAT A STORY! PRISON WALL DYNAMITED-FOUR GUARDS KILLED-AND THREE NOTORIOUS GANGSTERS ESCAPED.
J.J. LANE LEANS FORWARD, LOOKING A TRIFLE PALE.
EH? WHAT ARE THEIR NAMES?
IRON-JAW LADRONI, GANG LEADER, AND-LET'S SEE-A FELLA NAMED HUSH WATSON, AND-
WHY, DADDY! WHAT'S WRONG?
!
HE'S FAINTED!!
© 1934 BY NEA SERVICE, INC. T. M. REG. U. S. PAT. OFF.

SO SENSATIONAL IS THE PRISON BREAK, THAT WITHIN HALF AN HOUR THE POLICE OF FIVE STATES ARE BLOCKING EVERY MAIN HIGHWAY.
BUT THE CAREFULLY PLANNED GET-AWAY MOVES LIKE CLOCKWORK. THE GANGSTERS CHANGE FROM CAR TO TRUCK TO AIRPLANE.
HELLO, SAP. IT'S A STICK-UP.
AND, A FEW HOURS LATER, BRAZENLY HOLD UP A SHERIFF'S OFFICE HUNDREDS OF MILES AWAY...
......ESCAPING WITH A VALUABLE STORE OF SUB-MACHINE GUNS, AMMUNITION, TEAR GAS BOMBS, BULLET PROOF VESTS, AND GAS MASKS.
© 1934 BY NEA SERVICE, INC. T. M. REG. U. S. PAT. OFF.
Roy Crane

WANTED: DEAD OR ALIVE!
$5,000 REWARD OFFERED FOR CAPTURE OF IRON-JAW LADRONI.
SENSATIONAL PRISON BREAK AND HOLD-UP AROUSE NATION.
POLICE COMB UNDERWORLD. THE HUNT IS ON.
DIDN'T YOU SEE THAT STOP SIGN?
TWO DAYS PASS WITHOUT ANY NEWS. THEN, IN NEW YORK STATE, A POLICEMAN STOPS A CAR FOR A TRAFFIC VIOLATION.
HE GIVES THE OCCUPANTS A HARD-BOILED GLARE—THEN UTTERS A STARTLED GASP!
LADRONI!
LET 'IM HAVE IT, JOEY!
786341
T. M. REG. U. S. PAT. OFF.
© 1934 BY NEA SERVICE, INC.
Roy Crane
TWO SHOTS RING OUT—THE OFFICER FALLS— THE GANGSTER CAR SPEEDS AWAY. THE ENTIRE NATION ECHOES THE CRY, "GET LADRONI."

LADRONI ELUDES POLICE AGAIN!
SHOOTS OFFICER IN LATEST ESCAPADE.
MEANWHILE, ON THE PRETEXT OF OPENING A BANK ACCOUNT, EASY LOOKS OVER J. J. LANE'S BANK.
WHY ALL THE COPS HANGING AROUND? EXPECTING TROUBLE?
OH, NO INDEED, SIR!
© 1934 BY NEA SERVICE, INC. T. M. REG. U. S. PAT. OFF.
Roy Crane
BUT WITH ALL THOSE GANGSTERS AT LARGE, MR. LANE BELIEVES THE DEPOSITORS WILL FEEL SAFER WITH A NUMBER OF POLICE ON HAND.
SURE, I GET YOU.

77

10:15 A.M. SEVERAL WELL-DRESSED YOUNG MEN EMERGE FROM TWO CARS IN FRONT OF LANE'S BANK.
WASH AND EASY, STANDING NEAR BY, BARELY NOTICE THEM.
THE THING FOR US TO DO, PODNER, IS TO FIND OUT WHO THE OLD MAN'S BLONDE IS.
YEH.
BUM! BUM! BOOM!
SUDDENLY, THEY ARE STARTLED BY THREE MUFFLED EXPLOSIONS FROM WITHIN THE BANK.
THEY ARE ABOUT TO INVESTIGATE, WHEN ONE OF THE WELL-DRESSED YOUNG MEN----
MIND YER OWN BUSINESS, STUPID!
!
!
Roy Crane
© 1934 BY NEA SERVICE, INC. T. M. REG. U. S. PAT. OFF.

FOLLOWING THE EXPLOSIONS, MEN AND WOMEN POUR OUT OF THE BANK, GASPING AND CHOKING FOR BREATH.
FOUR ARMED MEN ADJUST GAS MASKS AND ENTER.
THE RATTLE OF A MACHINE GUN ECHOES FROM THE DEPTHS OF THE BANK. A CROWD GATHERS. SOMEONE SCREAMS.
IRON-JAW LADRONI! POLICE! POLICE!
ONLY EASY SEEMS TO HAVE THE PRESENCE OF MIND TO DO ANYTHING.
QUICK, MAN! LOAN ME A PISTOL.
!
© 1934 BY NEA SERVICE, INC. T. M. REG. U. S. PAT. OFF.
Roy Crane

June 1934

STILL UNHURRIED, THE GANGSTERS EMERGE FROM THE BANK, REMOVE THEIR GAS MASKS AND PANIC THE CROWD WITH BURSTS OF MACHINE GUN FIRE INTO THE AIR.
LOOK OUT! DON'T SHOOT!
THEN, HOLDING FRIGHTENED GIRLS AS SHIELDS, THE DESPERADOES SPEED AWAY.
HOT ON THEIR TRAIL, AND WITH SIRENS SCREAMING, COME THREE POLICE CARS.
© 1934 BY NEA SERVICE, INC. T. M. REG. U. S. PAT. OFF.
Roy Crane
ARMED CITIZENS, INCLUDING WASH AND EASY, HOP INTO OTHER CARS. THE CHASE IS ON!

79

WHO'S THE PATIENT?
MR. LANE. THIS WAY, DOCTOR. HE'S IN HIS PRIVATE OFFICE.
WE FOUND HIM JUST LIKE THIS. NOBODY SAW IT HAPPEN. I SUPPOSE ONE OF THOSE GANGSTERS SLUGGED HIM.
MMM!
I THINK, WILLIAMS, YOU'D PETTER SUMMON THE POLICE.
WHY? IS HE BADLY HURT?
J. J. LANE IS DEAD!
!
ROY CRANE
© 1934 BY NEA SERVICE, INC. T. M. REG. U. S. PAT. OFF.
BANKER DIES!
J. J. LANE FOUND DEAD IN PRIVATE OFFICE, FOLLOWING ROBBERY.
EMPLOYEES STUNNED AT DISCOVERY; NOTIFY POLICE.
WHAT DO YOU MAKE OF IT, DOC?
SHOT AT CLOSE RANGE, IN THE BASE OF THE SKULL. SMALL CALIBER. PROBABLY A .22.
ANOTHER NOTCH FOR LADRONI, EH?
AW, WHO EVER HEARD OF GANGSTERS USING A .22?
HUM! HOW LONG WOULD YOU SAY HE'S BEEN DEAD, DOC?
OH, ABOUT AN HOUR. MAYBE LONGER.
GREAT SCOTT! WHY, THAT MEANS HE DIED AT LEAST 20 MINUTES BEFORE LADRONI GOT HERE.
NOW, NOW. KELLY! I CAN'T BE POSITIVE. NOBODY CAN! MAYBE AN HOUR— MAYBE HALF AN HOUR. IT'S ONLY A GUESS.
ROY CRANE
T. M. REG. U. S. PAT. OFF. © 1934 BY NEA SERVICE, INC.
LET'S REASON THIS OUT, BOYS. SINCE LANE WAS SHOT WITH A .22, IT'S NOT LIKELY THE LADRONI MOB DID IT.
NAH. THEY'D USE A .38 OR .45. SAY, MAYBE HE COMMITTED SUICIDE.
HUMPH! AND HID THE GUN BEFORE DROPPING DEAD. THAT'S A SWELL EXPLANATION.
ULP!
TO CONTINUE, BOYS, IT'S A MURDER. J. J. LANE WAS SHOT DOWN IN COLD BLOOD, PERHAPS EVEN BEFORE THE HOLD-UP.
WHAT! YOU DON'T THINK THERE'S A CONNECTION BETWEEN THE HOLDUP AND THE KILLING?
NONE WHATSOEVER— UNLESS, OF COURSE, SOME ENEMY IN THE BANK, KNOWING A HOLD-UP WAS IN PROGRESS, AND HOPING THE GANGSTERS WOULD BE BLAMED, HASTILY CHOSE THAT VERY MOMENT FOR HIS CRIME.
© 1934 BY NEA SERVICE, INC. T. M. REG. U. S. PAT. OFF.

81

AND THIS IS MR. GRUFF, OUR CASHIER.
HUMPH! TRYING TO SOLVE OUR LITTLE MYSTERY TOO, EH?
YES, SUH.
WHAT'S THE MATTER WITH HIS HAND?
I BELIEVE HE BROKE IT, SIR.
FIGHTING, EH?
YES, SIR — I MEAN NO, SIR. I THINK HE FELL DOWN, SIR.
WELL, MAKE UP YOUR MIND! DID HE BREAK IT IN A FIGHT WITH J. J. LANE?
I DON'T KNOW, SIR. HONEST, I—THAT IS, I HEARD SOME OF THE BOYS TALKING, SIR, BUT I DIDN'T SEE IT.
© 1934 BY NEA SERVICE, INC. T. M. REG. U. S. PAT. OFF.
YEAH, THE CHIEF PHONED ME ABOUT YOU. I'M SERGEANT GRADY. PAT GRADY. GLAD TO COOPERATE ANY WAY I CAN.
THANKS.
QUEER CASE. LOOKS LIKE A SET-UP, AT FIRST. BY THE WAY, EVER HEAR OF A MAN NAMED RAYMOND POTTS?
NO, SUH.
RECOGNIZE THIS PICTURE?
SURE. THAT'S THE LANE'S HIRED MAN.
YEAH. HE'S THE FELLA WHO WASHED TH' FINGER PRINTS OFF THEIR SAFE. HIS NAME'S JOE TUCKER.
TUCKER, MY EYE! THAT'S POTTS! HE'S AN EX-BOOTLEGGER. THE GAL AT THE TELEPHONE DESK IS POSITIVE HE CALLED ON LANE JUST BEFORE THE MURDER.
© 1934 BY NEA SERVICE, INC. T. M. REG. U. S. PAT. OFF.
SAY! THAT'S A REAL CLUE.
I'LL SAY IT IS. LANE'S HIRED MAN, WITH A SHADY PAST AND USING AN ASSUMED NAME, COMES TO LANE'S OFFICE SHORTLY BEFORE LANE IS MURDERED.
GANGWAY! THIS IS MY BUSY DAY.
MORNIN', MISS LANE. I CAME FOR A TALK WITH YOUR HIRED MAN.
WHY, JOE ISN'T HERE.
IT'S THE STRANGEST THING. HE AND THE COOK SEEMED TERRIBLY UPSET OVER DADDY'S DEATH, AND LAST NIGHT THEY PACKED THEIR THINGS AND LEFT, WITHOUT EVEN SAYING, "GOODBY."
!

83

I RECKON YOU REMEMBER THE NIGHT, MISS DIAMOND, THAT WASH AND I PICKED YOU AND J.J. LANE UP IN A TAXI?
WELL! WHAT OF IT?
NOTHING, ONLY THERE ARE SEVERAL QUESTIONS I—
LISTEN, WISE GUY. I'VE TOLD ALL I KNOW— I'M SICK OF QUESTIONS. FIRST IT'S THE COPS, AND NOW IT'S YOU.
BUT—
TAKE A WALK, WILL YA? I DIDN'T HEAR ANY SHOTS. I DON'T KNOW ANYTHING ABOUT THE MURDER. I WASN'T EVEN IN THE BANK WHEN IT HAPPENED.
© 1934 BY NEA SERVICE, INC. T. M. REG. U. S. PAT. OFF.
DID YOU TELL THE POLICE ABOUT BEING SHADOWED WHEN YOU STEPPED OUT WITH J.J. LANE?
IT'S NONE OF YOUR COCK-EYED BUSINESS! GET ME?

THE BABY-FACED BLOND WON'T TALK, GRADY. ASKED HER SOME QUESTIONS ABOUT THE MURDER, AND SHE BLEW UP LIKE A FIRECRACKER.
YEAH. THAT'S BABE DIAMOND, THE OLD MAN'S SECRETARY.
BIN AROUND, THAT DAME. USED TO BE A NIGHT CLUB HOSTESS. MARRIED TWICE. HAS A NINE YEAR OLD KID IN FRISCO, AND CLAIMS SHE WAS ENGAGED TO MARRY LANE.
WHAT! ENGAGED TO MARRY J.J. LANE?
SOUNDS KINDA FISHY, I ADMIT. BUT SHE'S WEARIN' A BIG DIAMOND RING, AND HE PAID THE BILL. WE MADE SURE OF THAT.
© 1934 BY NEA SERVICE, INC. T. M. REG. U. S. PAT. OFF.
HECK! YOU CAN'T PIN NOTHIN' ON THAT DAME. WE'VE CHECKED EVERYTHING, AND SHE HAS WOT LOOKS TO BE A GOOD ALIBI.
MAYBE SO, BUT I'M GOING TO KEEP AN EYE ON HER.

LISTEN, GRADY, I'M SUSPICIOUS OF THAT BABE DIAMOND.
YOU CAN'T PIN NOTHIN' ON HER, THO. AT THE TIME LANE WAS S'POSED TO OF BEEN SHOT, SHE WAS OUT SHOPPING, AND CAN PROVE IT.
JUST THE SAME, I'D SURE LIKE TO LOOK OVER HER APARTMENT.
SURE, GO AHEAD. I'LL EVEN GIVE YOU A KEY.
BUT, WILL IT FIT HER DOOR?
YEAH. BURNS AND I WAS UP THERE THE OTHER DAY. BUT DON'T LET THAT STOP YOU, BOY. WE MIGHT OF MISSED SOMETHING.
TWENTY MINUTES LATER, WASH AND EASY ARE IN BABE'S APARTMENT.
HUM! PRETTY CLASSY, FOR A SECRETARY.
T. M. REG. U. S. PAT. OFF.
© 1934 BY NEA SERVICE, INC.

FIND ANYTHING ?
DUNNO, PODNER. IT'S THE WRAPPER OF A PACKAGE MAILED TO BABE DIAMOND ON THE DAY OF THE MURDER.
THE DATE'S PROBABLY JUST A COINCIDENCE, BUT— BLAZES! LOOK! WHY, IT'S ADDRESSED IN HER OWN HANDWRITING.
BUT WHY WOULD SHE MAIL SOME-THING TO HERSELF? 'AT'S WOT I CAN'T FIGGER OUT.
HEY, GRADY! JUST FOUND SOME EVIDENCE AGAINST BABE DIAMOND. ON THE DAY OF THE MURDER SHE—
FORGET IT, BOY.
FORGET IT. IT'S ALL OVER BUT THE SHOOTING. WE'VE FOUND THE PISTOL LANE WAS SHOT WITH, AND ARRESTED THE CASHIER.
© 1934 BY NEA SERVICE, INC. T. M. REG. U. S. PAT. OFF.
WHAT! YOU ARRESTED THE CASHIER?
YEAH, LOOKIT THE PAPERS. BOY WOTTA STORY!
CASHIER ACCUSED OF BANK MURDER
DID HE CONFESS, GRADY?
NAW, BUT HE WILL BEFORE BURNS GETS THRU WITH 'IM. Y'SEE, BOYS, LANE AND GRUFF, THE CASHIER, WERE ENEMIES. BEEN THAT WAY FOR WEEKS.
THEY HAD A FIGHT, TOO.
YEAH, THAT WAS WHEN LANE DEMANDED GRUFF'S RESIGNATION. GRUFF REFUSED. LOCKED THE DOOR BETWEEN THEIR OFFICES. OF COURSE WE SUSPECTED GRUFF, BUT WE WASN'T SURE.
© 1934 BY NEA SERVICE, INC. T. M. REG. U. S. PAT. OFF.
WELL, SIR, TODAY BURNS FOUND A .22 PISTOL HID IN GRUFF'S FILING CABINET. GRUFF ADMITS IT'S HIS AND, WHAT'S MORE, OUR BALLISTICS EXPERT SAYS POSITIVELY IT'S THE GUN THAT KILLED J. J. LANE.
?
WELL, ARE YOU SATISFIED IT WAS THE CASHIER WHO KILLED LANE?
HUM! I DUNNO, GRADY. WERE HIS FINGERPRINTS FOUND ON THE PISTOL?
WELL, NO. THERE WEREN'T ANY FINGERPRINTS AT ALL. OH, I ADMIT WE HAVEN'T PROOF THAT HE ACTUALLY FIRED THE SHOT.
BUT, HANG IT ALL, MAN! HE WAS LANE'S ENEMY. HE ADMITS THE GUN'S HIS. IT WAS FOUND IN HIS FILING CASE, AND HE'S GOT A BUM ALIBI. WHAT MORE DO YOU WANT?
A CONFESSION. UNTIL HE CONFESSES, GRADY, I'M STILL SUSPICIOUS OF A LOT O' PEOPLE.
YEAH, I KNOW. BABE DIAMOND. YOU THINK SHE'S DUMB ENOUGH TO BUMP OFF A FIANCE WORTH A COOL MILLION, ON THE EVE OF HER WEDDING. BALONEY!
© 1934 BY NEA SERVICE, INC. T. M. REG. U. S. PAT. OFF.

86

BIRTHDAY PRESENT FOR YOU, BETTY.
WHY, EASY! YOU OLD ANGEL
YOU HAVE NO IDEA WHAT A SURPRISE IT IS. YOU SEE, MY BIRTHDAY CAME ON THE VERY DAY DADDY WAS KILLED, AND I GOT ONLY ONE PRESENT.
FROM YOUR DAD?
NO, FROM AUNT ELLEN. DADDY HAD BEEN JOKING ABOUT WHAT A GRAND, PRESENT HE HAD FOR ME, BUT, POOR DEAR, HE DIED BEFORE EVER LEARNED WHAT IT WAS.
© 1934 BY NEA SERVICE, INC. T. M. REG. U. S. PAT. OFF.
THANKS, BETTY. THAT'S WHAT I WANTED TO KNOW. THE MURDER MYSTERY'S SOLVED.
?

WHAT?
I TELL YOU, BETTY, THE MURDER'S BEEN SOLVED. I KNOW WHO KILLED YOUR DAD.
WHO?
CAN'T TELL YOU NOW. IN A HURRY. QUICK—LOAN ME YOUR CAR.
EASY ROARS OUT OF THE LANE'S DRIVE AND DOWN THE STREET AT NEARLY 60 MILES AN HOUR.
HEY! YOU'LL GO TO JAIL FOR THIS!
STEP ON IT, BUDDIE. THAT'S EXACTLY WHERE I'M HEADING.
© 1934 BY NEA SERVICE, INC. T. M. REG. U. S. PAT. OFF.

HEY, GRADY! HERE'S A SPEED-HOUND WHO CLAIMS HE KNOWS WHO KILLED J. J. LANE.
IS ZAT SO?
?
GRADY AND EASY STEP ASIDE, AND FOR TEN MINUTES THE DETECTIVE LISTENS, SPELLBOUND.
HOLD ON, BOY! THIS LOOKS LIKE BIG STUFF. HEY, MABEL! GIMME THE DISTRICT ATTORNEY.
© 1934 BY NEA SERVICE, INC. T. M. REG. U. S. PAT. OFF.
FIVE MINUTES LATER, THE D.A., THE CHIEF OF POLICE, THE BANK CASHIER, EASY, AND GRADY ARE IN SECRET CONFERENCE.
I GOT MY ORDERS, BUDDIE. NOBODY—NOT EVEN THE MAYOR, CAN GIT IN.
J.V. PUTNEY
DIST. ATTORNEY
PRIVATE

July 1934

88

89

SHE'S STILL ALIVE, CHIEF, BUT I'M AFRAID SHE'S DONE FOR.
GET A DOCTOR.
WHILE THE POLICE, SURROUNDING THE SANITARIUM, ARE SHOOTING UP THE LADRONI MOB, THOSE INSIDE TURN TO THE WOMAN.
WHO'S DA DAME? LADRONI'S MOLL?
IT'S A SECRET, BUDDIE, BUT SINCE YOU GOT A KIND FACE, I'LL LET YOU IN ON IT.
HER NAME'S BABE DIAMOND.
WHO DA HECK'S BABE DIAMOND?
© 1934 BY NEA SERV INC. T. M. REG. U. S. PAT. OFF.
BABE, MY FRIEND, IS THE MURDERER OF J.J. LANE.
!?
WELL, THERE GOES THE LAST OF THE LADRONI MOB. THEY SHOT IT OUT ONCE TOO OFTEN.
JUST SOME MORE WISE GUYS WHO THOUGHT THEY COULD BEAT THE LAW, EH, CHIEF?
BOYS, I'M PROUD OF YOU.
THE RULE OF CROOKS IS A DISGRACE TO OUR LAND. THEIR YEARLY PLUNDER COSTS EACH FAMILY IN AMERICA $135. RACKETEERS, ALONE, ROB US OF ENOUGH TO BUY EVERY MAN AND BOY IN THE UNITED STATES A NEW HAT AND A SUIT OF CLOTHES.
I TELL YOU, GENTLEMEN, IT'S A DISGRACE. AND I'M PROUD TO BE AN HONEST COP WHO IS STRIVING TO RID AMERICA OF SUCH SNEAKS, SCOUNDRELS, AND KILLERS.
WELL, BOY, IT'S ALL OVER. WE'VE WIPED OUT A MOB OF GANGSTERS, SOLVED A MURDER MYSTERY, AND RUN DOWN AN UNDERCOVER HOSPITAL FOR CROOKS. WE OWE EVERYTHING TO YOU.
I WAS LUCKY, SUH.
EASY RIDES BACK TO TOWN WITH THE DISTRICT ATTORNEY AND THE CHIEF OF POLICE.
NONSENSE! AH! HERE ARE THE REPORTERS AND CAMERAMEN. COME ON, BOY, I'LL SEE THAT YOUR PICTURE GETS IN EVERY PAPER IN AMERICA.
HEY! WHERE'D HE GO? WHERE'S EASY?
MY STARS! HE MUST OF SKIPPED. HE'S THE FIRST GUY I EVER SAW WHO DIDN'T WANT TO BE A HERO.

HELLO, BETTY.
WHY, EASY! YOU OLD HERO! I'VE JUST BEEN READING HOW YOU SOLVED THE—THE MURDER.
HONEST, I THINK YOU'RE SIMPLY SWELL. WILL YOU TELL ME HOW YOU DID IT?
WITH PLEASURE.
BUT FIRST LET ME GIVE YOU THE BIRTHDAY PRESENT YOUR DAD BOUGHT, BUT NEVER HAD THE OPPORTUNITY OF GIVING YOU.
A DIAMOND RING!
© 1934 BY NEA SERVICE, INC. T. M. REG. U. S. PAT. OFF.
ROY CRANE
IT FITS PERFECTLY. WHY, WHERE ON EARTH DID YOU FIND IT?
ON BABE DIAMOND. YOU SEE, AFTER SHOOTING YOUR DAD, SHE TOOK THE RING TO DIVERT SUSPICION. SAID HE GAVE IT TO HER AS AN ENGAGEMENT RING. WE BELIEVED HER STORY UNTIL THE VERY LAST.

TELL ME, EASY, DID DADDY EVER DO ANYTHING—WELL, ANYTHING WRONG?
NEVER! HIS ONLY MISTAKE, BETTY, WAS IN HELPING TWO QUESTIONABLE PEOPLE EARN AN HONEST LIVING.
BABE DIAMOND WAS ONE. JOE, THE GARDENER, WAS THE OTHER. BABE WASN'T REALLY BAD—ONCE SHE WAS LADRONI'S MOLL, BUT WANTED TO GO STRAIGHT. KNOWING THIS, LANE GAVE HER A JOB.
OCCASSIONALLY TOOK HER TO DINNER. JOE, THE GARDENER, FOUND THIS OUT, AND, KNOWING BABE HAD BEEN A CROOK, TRIED TO BLACKMAIL YOUR DAD BY 'PHONE. WELL, LADRONI SHOT HIS WAY OUT OF PRISON—LOOKED UP BABE—FORCED HER TO TIP HIS GANG ON THE PROPER TIME FOR A BANK HOLD-UP.
ROY CRANE
© 1934 BY NEA SERVICE, INC. T. M. REG. U. S. PAT. OFF.
BABE GAVE A TIP BY LONG DISTANCE. WAS CAUGHT IN THE ACT BY LANE, AND, IN PANIC, SHOT LANE. THAT'S THE STORY.

BUT, EASY, DIDN'T THE POLICE THINK IT WAS THE CASHIER WHO KILLED DADDY?
SURE, HIS PISTOL FIRED THE FATAL SHOT, AND THEY WERE ENEMIES.
GEE! THAT LOOKED SUSPICIOUS!
OF COURSE, BUT I FIGURED THAT NOBODY BUT A FOOL WOULD TAKE HIS OWN PISTOL, SHOOT HIS ENEMY, IN AN ADJOINING ROOM, AND THEN REPLACE THE PISTOL IN HIS OWN FILING CABINET.
THAT'S TRUE.
AND THE CASHIER'S NO FOOL. THEREFORE, SOMEBODY ELSE MUST HAVE BORROWED THAT PISTOL, KILLED LANE, AND PURPOSELY REPLACED IT IN THE CASHIERS OFFICE WHERE IT WOULD BE FOUND.
ROY CRANE
SPLENDID! BUT HOW DID YOU GUESS THAT BABE DIAMOND DID IT?
I LEARNED THAT BABE, FOR SOME REASON, MAILED THE PISTOL AWAY FROM THE BANK. HENCE, SHE MUST O' BEEN THE ONE WHO PLANTED IT.

GEE, EASY, YOU'RE A WHIZ! BUT HOW'D YOU LEARN THAT BABE MAILED THE PISTOL AWAY FROM THE BANK?
I FOUND THE WRAPPER OF THE PACKAGE— IT WAS THE KEY TO THE ENTIRE SOLUTION.
ONLY THE WRAPPER?
YES, ADDRESSED IN HER HAND, AND SENT FIRST CLASS TO HER APARTMENT. WHEN QUESTIONED, SHE SAID THE PACKAGE CONTAINED A PAIR OF STEP-INS.
BABE, BEING A SECRETARY, KNEW THAT FIRST CLASS MAIL IS 2¢ AN OUNCE. NOW, GET THIS— STEP-INS CAN BE MAILED FOR ABOUT 6¢, YET THERE WAS 34¢ WORTH OF STAMPS ON THE WRAPPER. WHY?
WELL, I FIGURED THERE MUST O' BEEN A REASON. I WEIGHED THE PISTOL. 14 OUNCES. 28¢ FOR MAILING PISTOL, PLUS 6¢ FOR STEP-INS, EQUALS 34¢, THE AMOUNT ON THE PACKAGE.
!
© 1934 BY NEA SERVICE, INC., T. M. REG. U. S. PAT. OFF.

THE CASE AGAINST BABE WAS A CINCH AFTER I FOUND SHE'D MAILED THE PISTOL FROM THE BANK. I CHECKED PICTURES OF THE LADRONI MOB, AND LONG DISTANCE CALLS MADE FROM THE BANK.
WHAT'D YOU FIND?
THAT, ON THE DAY OF THE HOLD-UP, BABE 'PHONED A JOE POLAND IN WINCHESTER. THAT POLAND— HIS REAL NAME WAS POLARIS— WAS A MEMBER OF THE LADRONI MOB.
PRESTO! THAT LINKED BABE WITH LADRONI. SHE WAS THE TIP OFF. A CROOK. YET SHE CLAIMED TO BE ENGAGED TO MARRY YOUR DAD.
HOWEVER, HER "ENGAGEMENT" RING WAS REALLY A DINNER RING, AND FAR TOO BIG. OBVIOUSLY, SHE HAD STOLEN THE BIRTHDAY PRESENT YOUR DAD HAD BOUGHT FOR YOU. SO I PUT TWO AND TWO TOGETHER, AND THE MURDER WAS SOLVED.
GEE! IT SOUNDS SO EASY WHEN YOU EXPLAIN IT.

AFTER YOU EXPLAINED TO THE POLICE HOW BABE DIAMOND SHOT MY DADDY, WHY ON EARTH DID THEY ACCUSE THE CASHIER?
THAT WAS THE CHIEF'S IDEA.
HE WANTED TO NAB LADRONI, BUT DIDN'T KNOW WHERE TO FIND HIM. BABE, HE THOUGHT, WOULD GO TO HIM THE MOMENT SHE FELT THAT THE POLICE WERE NO LONGER WATCHING HER.
THE CASHIER FELL IN WITH THE IDEA, LET 'EM ACCUSE HIM OF THE MURDER, AND PRESTO! BABE LED THE WAY TO LADRONI, WHO WAS RECOVERING FROM WOUNDS HE'D RECEIVED IN THE BANK HOLD-UP.
BUT WHY DID THOSE GANGSTERS SHOOT HER?
THEY WERE HAVING A BIG PAY-OFF, AND THOUGHT BABE HAD DOUBLE-CROSSED 'EM AND SQUEALED TO THE POLICE.
© 1934 BY NEA SERVICE, INC. T. M. REG. U. S. PAT. OFF.

BUT THE CHIEF OF POLICE IS IN CONFERENCE WITH THE MAYOR. ----WHAT?---- WHO?
WHO?
GET OUT! DIDN'T I TELL YOU, CASEY, THAT I'M IN CONFERENCE?
BUT CHIEF, IT'S HORATIO BOARDMAN.
!
WHO?
HORATIO BOARDMAN! HE'S OUTSIDE! HE'S WAITIN' TO SEE YOU.
HORATIO BOARDMAN! MY STARS! MY STARS! QUICK, JAKE, CLEAR THE BOTTLES. WHERE'S MY COAT? DON'T STAND THERE LIKE AN IDIOT, CASEY— SHOW MR. BOARDMAN IN.
?
23
ROY CRANE
AH, MR. BOARDMAN, YOUR VISIT IS INDEED AN HONOR.
IT IS A PLEASURE, SIR.
HUMPH! IT'S A DARN NUISANCE.
ER, YES, SIR. I QUITE AGREE, SIR.
DO BE SEATED, MR. BOARDMAN. HAVE A CIGAR.
?
WON'T YOU HAVE A CHAIR, SIR?
HUMPH! IF THE CHAIR'S NO BETTER'N YOUR CIGARS, I'LL STAND!
24
HEH, HEH! DROLL, ISN'T HE? ALWAYS JOKING.
AH—WHAT DID YOU THINK, SIR, OF THE WAY WE HANDLED THE LADRONI AFFAIR?
I DIDN'T COME HERE TO TELL WHAT I THINK. I CAME TO FIND OUT SOMETHING— WHO'S CAPTAIN EASY?
© 1934 BY NEA SERVICE, INC. T. M. REG. U. S. PAT. OFF.
ROY CRANE
EH? YOU WANT TO KNOW WHO CAPTAIN EASY IS, MR. BOARDMAN?
THAT'S WHAT I SAID. DON'T BEAT AROUND THE BUSH. I'M A BUSY MAN— A VERY BUSY MAN.
CHIEF OF POLICE
$5000 REWARD
WARD
HONESTY IS THE BEST POLICY
YES, SIR. WHY, AH, I THINK HE'S SORT OF A SOLDIER OF FORTUNE, SIR.
SO I GATHERED, FROM THE PAPERS. BUT WHO IS HE? WHAT'S HIS LAST NAME? WHERE'S HE BEEN? WHERE'S HE FROM?
MY STARS! WHY—AH—LET ME SEE---
BAH! I SEE THAT YOU KNOW NOTHING. ABSOLUTELY NOTHING!
CHIEF OF POLICE
$5000 REWARD
25
WELL, SIR, HE'S A HAPPY-GO-LUCKY, TWO-FISTED GUY WHO DOESN'T GIVE A WHOOP WHETHER HE EATS OR STARVES. HE'S A NUT. ALL HE CARES ABOUT IS THRILLS AND—
SPLENDID! SPLENDID! HE'S THE VERY CHAP I'VE BEEN LOOKING FOR.
CHIEF OF POLICE
$5000 REWARD
ROY CRANE

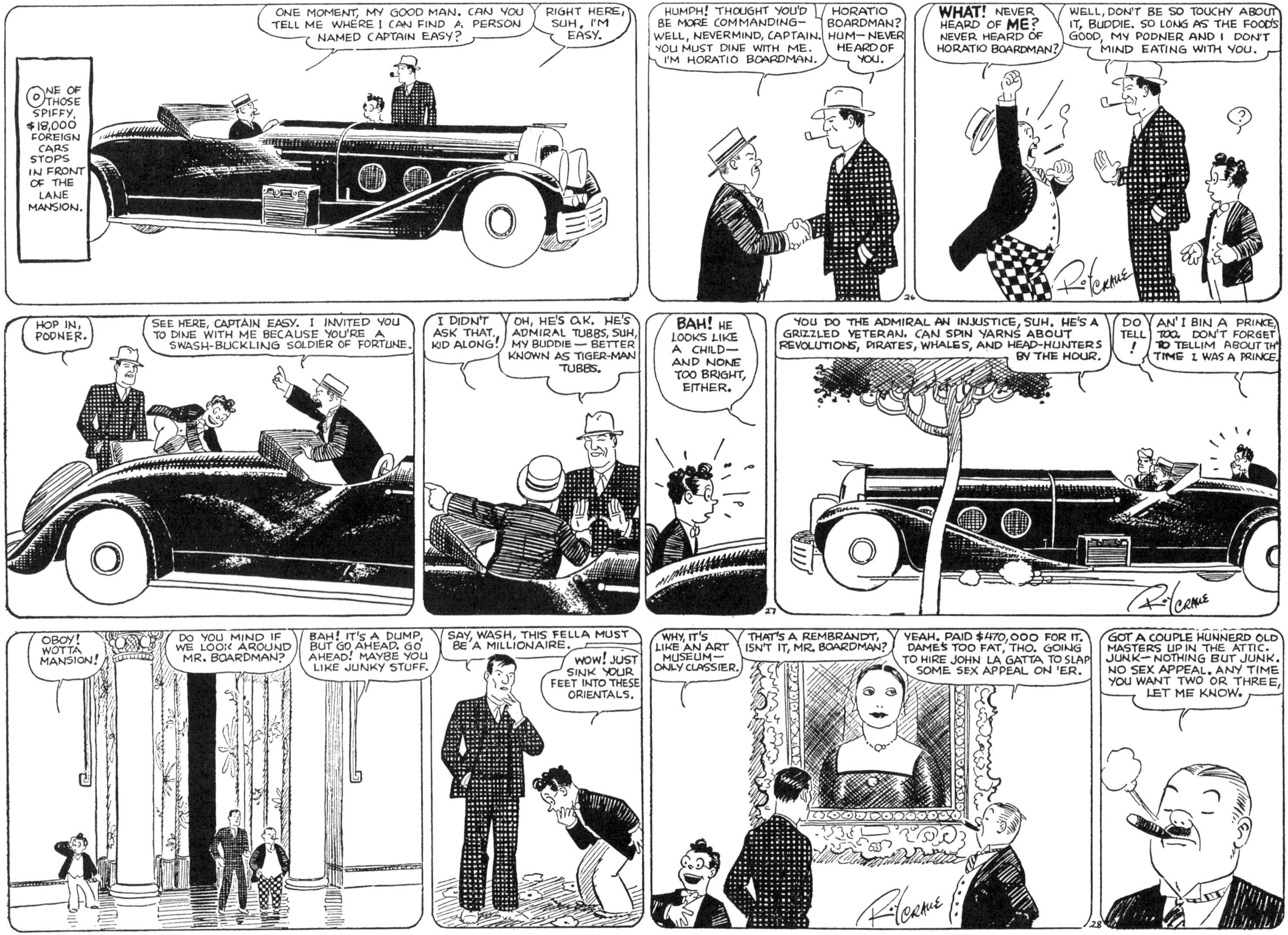
ONE OF THOSE SPIFFY, $18,000 FOREIGN CARS STOPS IN FRONT OF THE LANE MANSION.
ONE MOMENT, MY GOOD MAN. CAN YOU TELL ME WHERE I CAN FIND A PERSON NAMED CAPTAIN EASY?
RIGHT HERE, SUH, I'M EASY.
HUMPH! THOUGHT YOU'D BE MORE COMMANDING— WELL, NEVERMIND, CAPTAIN. YOU MUST DINE WITH ME. I'M HORATIO BOARDMAN.
HORATIO BOARDMAN? HUM— NEVER HEARD OF YOU.
WHAT! NEVER HEARD OF ME? NEVER HEARD OF HORATIO BOARDMAN?
WELL, DON'T BE SO TOUCHY ABOUT IT, BUDDIE. SO LONG AS THE FOOD'S GOOD, MY PODNER AND I DON'T MIND EATING WITH YOU.
?
HOP IN, PODNER.
SEE HERE, CAPTAIN EASY. I INVITED YOU TO DINE WITH ME BECAUSE YOU'RE A SWASH-BUCKLING SOLDIER OF FORTUNE.
I DIDN'T ASK THAT KID ALONG!
OH, HE'S O.K. HE'S ADMIRAL TUBBS, SUH, MY BUDDIE — BETTER KNOWN AS TIGER-MAN TUBBS.
BAH! HE LOOKS LIKE A CHILD— AND NONE TOO BRIGHT, EITHER.
YOU DO THE ADMIRAL AN INJUSTICE, SUH. HE'S A GRIZZLED VETERAN. CAN SPIN YARNS ABOUT REVOLUTIONS, PIRATES, WHALES, AND HEAD-HUNTERS BY THE HOUR.
DO TELL!
AN' I BIN A PRINCE, TOO. DON'T FORGET TO TELLIM ABOUT TH' TIME I WAS A PRINCE.
OBOY! WOTTA MANSION!
DO YOU MIND IF WE LOOK AROUND MR. BOARDMAN?
BAH! IT'S A DUMP, BUT GO AHEAD. GO AHEAD! MAYBE YOU LIKE JUNKY STUFF.
SAY, WASH, THIS FELLA MUST BE A MILLIONAIRE.
WOW! JUST SINK YOUR FEET INTO THESE ORIENTALS.
WHY, IT'S LIKE AN ART MUSEUM— ONLY CLASSIER.
THAT'S A REMBRANDT, ISN'T IT, MR. BOARDMAN?
YEAH. PAID $470,000 FOR IT. DAME'S TOO FAT, THO. GOING TO HIRE JOHN LA GATTA TO SLAP SOME SEX APPEAL ON 'ER.
GOT A COUPLE HUNNERD OLD MASTERS UP IN THE ATTIC. JUNK— NOTHING BUT JUNK. NO SEX APPEAL. ANY TIME YOU WANT TWO OR THREE, LET ME KNOW.

WELL, LET'S EAT. HEY, YOU— I CAN'T THINK OF YOUR NAME— WHERE'S ALL THE SERVANTS AT? WHERE'S THE FOOD? BRING ON THE WINE.
?
MM-M BOY! DELICIOUS! PERFECT!!
IT'S A RARE SIBERIAN GILLYFISH, SIR. MR. BOARDMAN HAS THEM SHIPPED ALIVE, SIR, BY SPECIAL PLANE.
GILLYFISH? WHAT, AGAIN? THROW THE CURSED STUFF OUT! IT'S IMPOSSIBLE! IMPOSSIBLE! I WANT SOMETHING FIT TO EAT. WHERE'S THE CHEF? WHY IN TARNATION DOES HE THINK I PAY HIM $30,000 A YEAR?
ROY CRANE
WELL, LET'S HOPE THE CIGARS ARE BETTER THAN THE DINNER. HELP YOURSELF, CAPTAIN. THEY'RE SPECIALLY MADE FOR ME BY A GENERAL IN THE CUBAN ARMY.
THANKS.
OBOY! MONOGRAMMED 'N' EVERYTHING.
WOTTA SMOKE!
SAY! THEY'RE PERFECT, MR. BOARDMAN
BAH!
WHAT'S THE MATTER?
TOO MOIST, AGAIN! HANG IT ALL—THEY'RE NEVER RIGHT! NOTHING'S ANY GOOD ANY MORE. NOTHING! I PAY TWO BUCKS APIECE FOR CIGARS, AND THEY AREN'T FIT TO SMOKE.
UH-EXCUSE ME, PLEASE
BAM! BAM!
TWO BUCKS APIECE! SAY, THAT GUY MUST BE CRAZY.
ROY CRANE
PERHAPS YOU'VE WONDERED, CAPTAIN, WHY I, A MILLIONAIRE, HAVE ASKED YOU TO DINNER.
WHY, YES, SUH, I HAVE.
WELL, IT'S THIS WAY. I UNDERSTAND YOU'RE A NUT. YOU GOT A CRAZY IDEA THAT THIS DIZZY WORLD WE LIVE IN IS JUST A BIG MERRY-GO-ROUND OF PLEASURE.
I GET A KICK OUT O' LIFE, IF THAT'S WHAT YOU MEAN.
EXACTLY! WHILE I— A MAN WHO HAS EVERYTHING LITERALLY EVERYTHING — AM BORED.
ROY CRANE
BORED WITH LIFE—DO YOU GET ME? EVERYTHING'S A PAIN IN THE NECK, AND I'LL GIVE $10,000 TO ANYBODY WHO CAN SHOW ME A GOOD TIME.
!

August 1934

WHAT! YOU'LL GIVE $10,000, TO ANYBODY WHO SHOWS YOU A GOOD TIME.
THAT'S WHAT I SAID. I'M BORED. EVERYTHING'S A PAIN IN THE NECK. I WANT TO ENJOY LIFE.
!
LET'S GET THIS STRAIGHT. IF WE SHOW YOU SOME FUN, YOU'LL GIVE US $10,000?
$10,000 CASH. FURTHERMORE, I'LL PAY ALL EXPENSES.
2
WHOOPEE! THE JOB'S OURS.
BOARDMAN, YOU'RE AS GOOD AS CURED. WE ACCEPT.
HUMPH!
© 1934 BY NEA SERVICE, INC. T. M. REG. U. S. PAT. OFF.
Roy Crane
IMAGINE A GUY LIKE HORATIO BOARDMAN! HE'S A MILLIONAIRE. HE HAS CASTLES AND MANSIONS AND VILLAS AND HUNTING LODGES ALL OVER THE WORLD
HE HAS PRIVATE TRAINS, AND YACHTS, AND MOTOR CARS GALORE.
HE OWNS RAILWAYS AND OIL FIELDS AND BANKS AND INDUSTRIAL ENTERPRISES BY THE DOZENS.
Roy Crane
© 1934 BY NEA SERVICE, INC. T. M. REG. U. S. PAT. OFF.
3
YET HE IS BORED WITH LIFE!
$10,000 HE OFFERS TO ANYONE WHO CAN SHOW HIM A GOOD TIME.
$10,000 IN CASH!
DO WASH AND EASY GIVE HIM THE HA-HA?
WE'LL TELL THE COCK-EYED WORLD THEY DON'T! THEY'RE GOING TO SHOW HORATIO BOARDMAN A GOOD TIME, IF IT TAKES 40 YEARS.
LUCKY BOARDMAN! THEY SAY HE BOUGHT THIS COW-PASTURE FOR $50.
GOLD, GOLD, GOLD! EVERYTHING HORATIO BOARDMAN TOUCHES TURNS TO GOLD.
FOR 20 YEARS HE'S INVESTED PENNIES AND REAPED MILLIONS. NOW, AT 42, HE'S TIRED OF MAKING MONEY.
BAH!
$
Roy Crane
HE'S TIRED OF HIS TOYS—HIS YACHTS, AND CASTLES, AND PRIVATE TRAINS. ANYTHING HE WANTS, HE BUYS.
4
HE HAS EVERYTHING! EVERYTHING BUT HAPPINESS!
AND, NOW, HE INTENDS TO BUY HAPPINESS.... HE INTENDS TO BUY IT LIKE SO MANY PORK CHOPS.
$10,000 IN CASH HE'LL PAY TO WASH AND EASY FOR A SINGLE GOOD TIME.

97

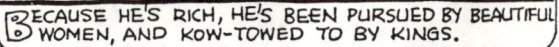

FOOEY ON THAT GUY! LET'S SCRAM! WE'RE WASTIN' OUR TIME TRYIN' TO SHOW OLD BOARDMAN A GOOD TIME.
WHY, YOU DUMPY DOODLE-BUG, YOU'RE A QUITTER—A SOFTIE. YOU HAVEN'T THE NERVE TO TACKLE A TOUGH JOB.
TH' HECK I HAVEN'T! I'M JUSTA WISE POTATO WHO KNOWS WHEN I'M LICKED, 'AT'S ALL.
LISTEN, SAP, WE'RE GOING TO MAKE A MAN OF BOARDMAN. AND WHETHER HE HAS A GOOD TIME, OR NOT, WE'RE GOING TO ENJOY A FREE VACATION
IT'S NO VACATION LISTENIN' TO HIM BELLYACHE.
© 1934 BY NEA SERVICE, INC. T. M. REG. U. S. PAT. OFF.
AW, FORGET IT. WE'VE BEEN WANTING TO GO FISHING, AND NOW'S OUR CHANCE. WE'LL DRAG THE OLD BOY UP TO ONE OF HIS PRIVATE LAKES, AND HAVE THE TIME OF OUR LIVES.
?

IT WORKED, PODNER. HE AGREED. OLD BOARDMAN AGREED TO GO ON A CAMPING TRIP.
YOU'RE KIDDIN'.
WIFE NO.5
WIFE NO.6
THE BATHER
HONEST TO HENRY! WE'RE GOING TO ONE OF HIS PRIVATE LAKES—IT'S A HUNDRED MILES FROM A PAVED ROAD, OR A POST OFFICE.
MY GOSH! WHY, WE'LL MAKE A MAN OUTA TH' OLD BOY YET.
YES, MR. BOARDMAN.
I'M GOING TO ROUGH IT IN THE WILDS, BAXTER. SEE THAT NO SERVANTS GO ALONG EXCEPT A CHEF, MY SECRETARY, AND MY VALET.
?
AND BY THE WAY, BAXTER, HAVE TWO AMPHIBIANS READY. SEE THAT THE CAMP IS PROPERLY EQUIPPED WITH HOT AND COLD WATER, REFRIGERATORS, AND ELECTRIC LIGHTS. NOTHING FANCY, MIND YOU—I'M GOING TO ROUGH IT.
PLOP!

SEE HERE, MR. BOARDMAN, WE WERE GOING TO ROUGH IT IN THE WOODS, AND HERE YOU'RE TAKING ALONG AIRPLANES, REFRIGERATORS, VALETS, AND—
WELL, WHAT OF IT? WHAT OF IT?
BLAZES! DON'T BE A SOFTIE. THAT'S NO WAY TO CAMP OUT.
HOW DARE YOU TELL ME HOW TO RUN MY OWN AFFAIRS?
GET THIS STRAIGHT, BOARDMAN. WE--
YOU LISTEN TO ME, YOU YOUNG WHIPPER-SNAPPER. MY NAME IS MISTER BOARDMAN—AND YOU'LL DO AS I SAY, OR GET OUT!
ONE O' THESE DAYS, PODNER, I'M GOING TO PUNCH THAT FELLA'S NOSE.
OH HO! GETTIN' SORE A'READY, EH? OBOY! YOU'RE TH' BOZO WHO WAS GUNNA ENJOY A SWELL VACATION, FREE.

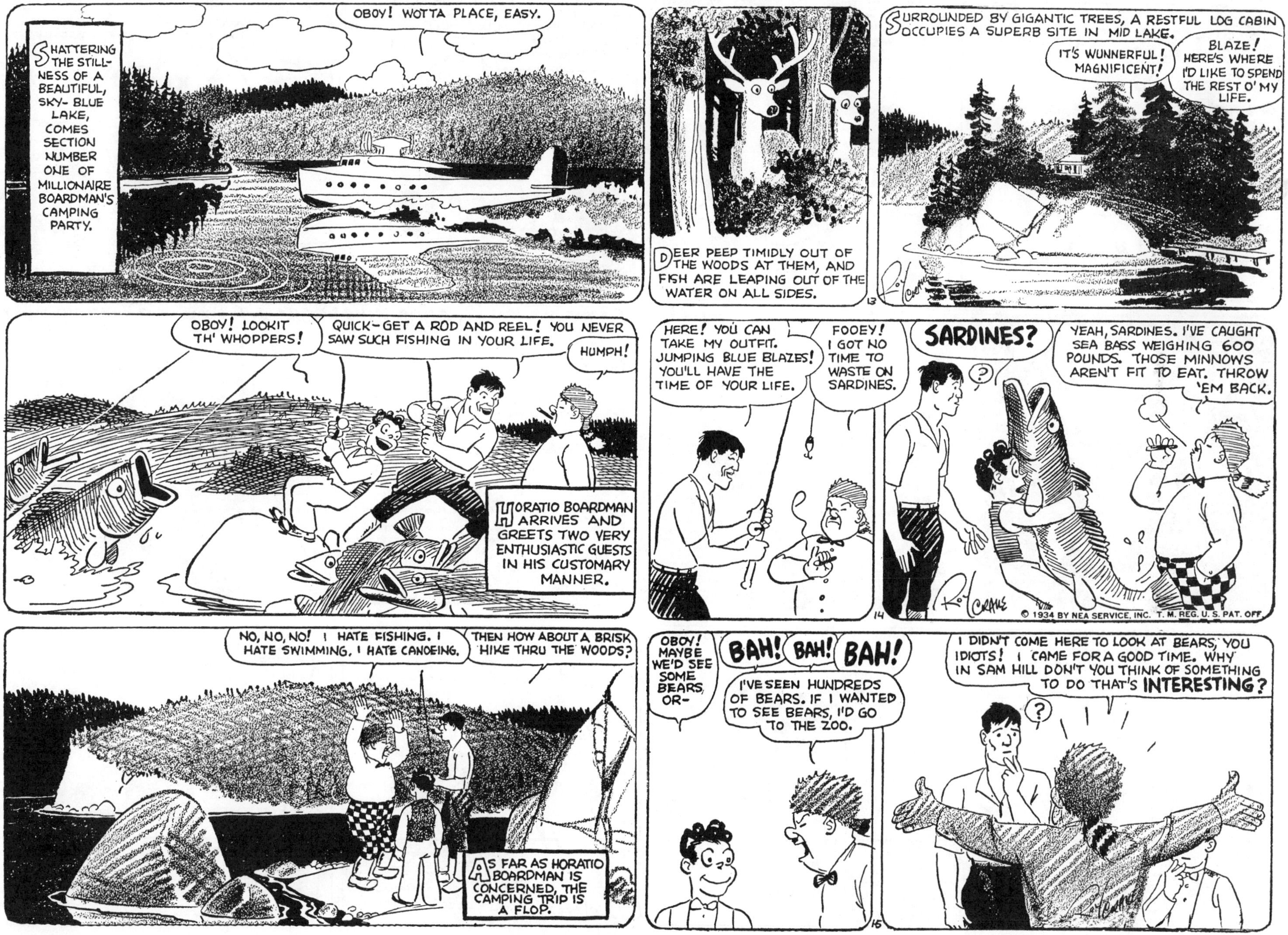

OBOY! WOTTA PLACE, EASY.
SHATTERING THE STILLNESS OF A BEAUTIFUL, SKY-BLUE LAKE, COMES SECTION NUMBER ONE OF MILLIONAIRE BOARDMAN'S CAMPING PARTY.
DEER PEEP TIMIDLY OUT OF THE WOODS AT THEM, AND FISH ARE LEAPING OUT OF THE WATER ON ALL SIDES.
13
SURROUNDED BY GIGANTIC TREES, A RESTFUL LOG CABIN OCCUPIES A SUPERB SITE IN MID LAKE.
IT'S WUNNERFUL! MAGNIFICENT!
BLAZE! HERE'S WHERE I'D LIKE TO SPEND THE REST O' MY LIFE.
OBOY! LOOKIT TH' WHOPPERS!
QUICK–GET A ROD AND REEL! YOU NEVER SAW SUCH FISHING IN YOUR LIFE.
HUMPH!
HORATIO BOARDMAN ARRIVES AND GREETS TWO VERY ENTHUSIASTIC GUESTS IN HIS CUSTOMARY MANNER.
HERE! YOU CAN TAKE MY OUTFIT. JUMPING BLUE BLAZES! YOU'LL HAVE THE TIME OF YOUR LIFE.
FOOEY! I GOT NO TIME TO WASTE ON SARDINES.
14
SARDINES?
?
YEAH, SARDINES. I'VE CAUGHT SEA BASS WEIGHING 600 POUNDS. THOSE MINNOWS AREN'T FIT TO EAT. THROW 'EM BACK.
© 1934 BY NEA SERVICE, INC. T. M. REG. U. S. PAT. OFF.
NO, NO, NO! I HATE FISHING. I HATE SWIMMING. I HATE CANOEING.
THEN HOW ABOUT A BRISK HIKE THRU THE WOODS?
AS FAR AS HORATIO BOARDMAN IS CONCERNED, THE CAMPING TRIP IS A FLOP.
OBOY! MAYBE WE'D SEE SOME BEARS, OR–
BAH! BAH! BAH!
I'VE SEEN HUNDREDS OF BEARS. IF I WANTED TO SEE BEARS, I'D GO TO THE ZOO.
15
I DIDN'T COME HERE TO LOOK AT BEARS, YOU IDIOTS! I CAME FOR A GOOD TIME. WHY IN SAM HILL DON'T YOU THINK OF SOMETHING TO DO THAT'S INTERESTING?
?

I'M DISTRACTED, SIR. MR. BOARDMAN COMPLAINS THAT IT'S TOO QUIET — HE CAN'T SLEEP AT NIGHT.
HOW 'BOUT BEATIN' A BASS DRUM OUTSIDE HIS WINDA?
16
PLEASE, MR. TUBBS. I'M SERIOUS. I'LL LOSE MY JOB, SIR, IF I DON'T DO SOMETHING.
WELL, YA MIGHT GET SOME HORSES, AN' PUT 'EM UP IN TH' ATTIC.
THERE SEEMS TO BE A SCARCITY OF BULLFROGS ON THE LAKE, SIR. DO YOU THINK IT WOULD HELP, SIR, IF I SENT AWAY FOR SOME LIVE FROGS?
OBOY! 'AT'S A SWELL IDEA.
PRESTO! ONE OF THE PLANES DEPARTS, AND RETURNS WITH 4000 JUMBO FROGS.
WOW! WOTTA RACKET!
HUH? I CAN'T HEAR YA FOR THESE DARN FROGS.
KA-ROAK! KA-ROAK!
BA-ROOM!
KA-ROAK!
KA-ROAK!
ROY CRANE

KA-ROAK! ka-roak! KA-ROAK! BA-ROOM! BA-ROOM BA-ROOM!
KA-ROAK! KA-ROAK!
BAXTER! BAXTER! WHAT ON EARTH IS MAKING THAT INFERNAL RACKET?
FROGS, SIR. YOU COMPLAINED THAT YOU COULDN'T SLEEP, SIR, AND I — AH — HAD 4000 BULLFROGS PUT INTO THE LAKE.
4000 BULLFROGS? YOU IMBECILE! THEY'RE ENOUGH TO WAKE THE DEAD. THEY'RE DRIVING ME CRAZY!
KA-ROAK! KA-ROAK! KA-ROAK!
ROY CRANE
© 1934 BY NEA SERVICE, INC. T. M. REG. U. S. PAT. OFF.
SHALL I GET RID OF THEM, SIR?
INSTANTLY, YOU FOOL, INSTANTLY! SHOOT 'EM! DROWN 'EM! DO ANYTHING TO STOP THAT INFERNAL NOISE, SO I CAN GO TO SLEEP.
17

YOU TELL THAT SOUR-FACED, OLD PICKLE TO KILL HIS OWN FROGS. I'LL BE HANGED IF I GET OUT O' BED AND—
PLEASE, PLEASE, CAPTAIN. MR. BOARDMAN'S USED TO HAVING HIS OWN WAY. HE CAN'T SLEEP. HE'S ORDERED US TO SHOOT EVERY FROG ON THE LAKE.
4,000 FROGS! GEE WIZ!
BANG! BANG! BANG! BANGBANGBANG! POWIE!
HEY! MORE SHELLS.
MORE SHELLS! SEND A PLANE AFTER MORE SHELLS.
HOLD ON! STOP THE SHOOTING.
BANG! BANGBANG! Wham! Blooey!
ROY CRANE
18
WHAT'S TH' MATTER, NOW?
MR. BOARDMAN CAN'T SLEEP, FOR THE SHOOTING.
HE COULDN'T SLEEP ANYWAY.
FIRST IT'S TOO QUIET—THEN IT'S TOO NOISY. MY GOSH! AIN'T THAT GUY EVER SATISFIED?
WOT HE NEEDS IS A POKE IN THE NOSE.
© 1934 BY NEA SERVICE, INC. T. M. REG. U. S. PAT. OFF.

WELL, BOYS, IT LOOKS LIKE MR. BOARDMAN'LL BE ABLE TO SLEEP IN SPITE OF THE FROGS. HE'S STUFFED. COTTON IN HIS EARS.
SHOO! 'AT WON'T HELP.
HE'LL THINK OF SOMETHING NEW TO CRAB ABOUT.
THERE! WOTTID I TELL YA?
HEY, BAXTER! WHAT IN HECK'S THE IDEA OF THIS MOSQUITO IN MY ROOM?
I CAN'T SLEEP. HE'S DRIVING ME CRAZY!
BAH! THAT GUY MUST LIE AWAKE NIGHTS THINKING UP NEW THINGS TO BEEF ABOUT.
IF THIS OLD WORLD'S SUCH A PAIN IN THE NECK, WHY THE BLAZES DOESN'T HE LAY DOWN AND DIE.
'AT WOULDN'T HELP, EASY. HE WOULDN'T LIKE HEAVEN, EITHER.

PODNER, I HAVE AN IDEA.
IF IT'S ANYTHING LIKE GIVIN' OLD BOARDMAN A POKE IN THE NOSE, I'M FOR IT.
IT'S EVEN BETTER. THERE'S AN ARABIAN PROVERB, SPORT, THAT TO ENJOY A FEATHER BED, A FELLA MUST FIRST SLEEP ON A ROCK PILE.
THAT'S BOARDMAN'S TROUBLE. HE'S NEVER SLEPT ON ROCKS. HE'S HAD IT TOO SOFT. FROM NOW ON, SPORT, WE'RE GOING TO GIVE 'IM SOMETHING TO REALLY CRAB ABOUT.
OBOY! YOU MEAN SUMPIN LIKE LOSIN' HIM IN A SWAMP FOR A COUPLA DAYS, WITH NOTHIN' T'EAT, AN' MILLIONS OF MOSQUITOES?
THAT'S THE IDEA, EXACTLY.

AH-GOOD MORNING, MR. BOARDMAN.
BAH!
FOOEY!
AREN'T YOU FEELIN' WELL?
I FEEL TERRIBLE. I ALWAYS FEEL TERRIBLE. I FEEL EVEN WORSE THAN USUAL.
NOT HAVIN' A GOOD TIME, EH?
BAH! I NEVER HAD SUCH A ROTTEN TIME IN MY LIFE. WHERE'S THE PLANE? I'M GOING HOME.
SPLAT! SWOP!
SORRY, SIR. ONE OF TH' PLANES JUST LEFT FOR NEW YORK TO GET TH' DAILY PAPER, AN' TH' OTHER ONE---
I TELL YOU, I WON'T STAY ANOTHER MINUTE. I'M SICK OF THE DUMP. D'YOU HEAR? I'M SICK OF IT!

HE SAYS HE'S SICKA TH' DUMP.
PLANE, OR NO PLANE, I WON'T STAY HERE ANOTHER MINUTE!
GOOD! WE'LL HOP IN A CANOE, AND GO PLACES.
WHAT! YOU EXPECT ME, AN OWNER OF PALATIAL YACHTS, TO RIDE IN A DINKY CANOE?
AW, JUMP IN!
IF I GO, I'LL NOT HAVE THIS PESKY BRAT TAGGING ALONG.
!
O.K., BUT YOU'LL HAVE TO PADDLE.
OH, VERY WELL, LET HIM STAY. BUT HE'S A DARNED PEST.
WELL, CAN YA BEAT THAT? OLD BOARDMAN'S IN A CANOE.
AND MR. TUBBS SAID THEY MIGHT BE GONE A MONTH.
23
© 1934 BY NEA SERVICE, INC. T. M. REG. U. S. PAT. OFF.

WHAT'S THE MATTER WITH THIS THING? HAVE YOU GOT THE ANCHOR OUT? WHY DON'T WE MOVE?
24
YOU CALL THIS SPEED? SHAKE A LEG. MY STARS! THIS IS THE POKIEST CONTRAPTION I WAS EVER IN.
HEY! WHERE YOU GOING? HELP! TURN AROUND! WE'LL BE DROWNED! WE'LL BE DASHED TO PIECES! GO BACK, YOU FOOLS! GO BACK!
TOO LATE NOW, SUH. WE THOUGHT YOU WANTED SPEED.
Roy Crane

STOP! HELP! LET ME OUT OF THIS CRAZY THING.
SIT DOWN! YOU'LL TURN US OVER!
HELP!
GLUB!
SPLASH!
GRAB 'IM, PODNER. HE CAN'T SWIM FOR SOUR APPLES.
25
THE OLD FOOL! WHY DIDN'T HE SET DOWN?
OH, HE STILL THINKS HE KNOWS IT ALL. HE'S A FRESHMAN JUST ENROLLING IN THE COLLEGE O' HARD KNOCKS.
Roy Crane

WHAT HAPPENED ?
YOU NEARLY DROWNED, 'AT'S WOT.
YOU WERE DUMB ENOUGH TO STAND UP WHILE SHOOTING THE RAPIDS.
WHERE'S THE CANOE? WHERE'S MY WATCH? WHY IN SAM HILL DIDN'T YOU SAVE MY WATCH?
CAN Y'BEAT IT? WE SAVE HIS LIFE, AN' HE CRABS ABOUT HIS WATCH.
DON'T STAND THERE, YOU IDIOTS! BUILD A FIRE. CAN'T YOU SEE I'M FREEZING?
THE MATCHES ARE WET.
WHAT! YOU MEAN I CAN'T SMOKE, OR DRY MY CLOTHES? IT'S AN OUTRAGE.
NOT ONLY THAT, SUH, BUT THERE'S NO FOOD, NO BEDS, NO CHEF, NO VALET, NO ELECTRIC LIGHTS.
27
FOR ONCE IN YOUR LIFE, BOARDMAN, YOU GOT SOMETHING TO CRAB ABOUT. WET CLOTHES, NO FIRE, NO FOOD, NO CANOE, NOT EVEN A VALET.
OH, MY STARS! MY STARS!
FURTHERMORE, IT'S 12 MILES BACK TO CAMP, OVER TH' ROUGHEST, WILDEST COUNTRY Y' EVER SAW.
IT'S ALL YOUR FAULT, YOU BRAINLESS IDIOTS!
YOU'RE FIRED! GET OUT! GET OUT! YOU'RE FIRED! YOU'RE THRU!
NOW, ISN'T THAT A SHAME.
BOARDMAN, YOU'RE BUSTING MY HEART.
28
T. M. REG. U. S. PAT. OFF.
GET OUT! YOU'RE FIRED!
WELL, WELL! THAT BEING THE CASE, PODNER, WE'LL LET MR. BOARDMAN FIND HIS OWN WAY BACK TO CAMP.
SURE, IT'S ONLY 12 MILES—JUST A NICE HIKE AN' A SWIM.
HE MIGHT GET LOST WADING THRU THAT TERRIBLE SWAMP, THO. DO YOU THINK HE'D MIND THE MOSQUITOES?
WELL, HE MIGHT GET PRETTY HUNGRY.
OH, HE WOULDN'T MIND THAT. HE DOESN'T ENJOY EATIN', ANYWAY.
THAT'S TRUE. AND IN CASE HE DOES GET HUNGRY, HE CAN ALWAYS KILL A BEAR.
SURE, ONLY HE'S SO PARTICULAR HE'D WANT IT COOKED.
WELL, SO LONG, SPORT. WATCH OUT FOR THE WILDCATS. AND IF YOU HAPPEN TO MISS THE CAMP, JUST KEEP GOING— THERE'S A ROAD ABOUT 40 MILES BEYOND.
29
© 1934 BY NEA SERVICE, INC. T. M. REG. U. S. PAT. OFF.

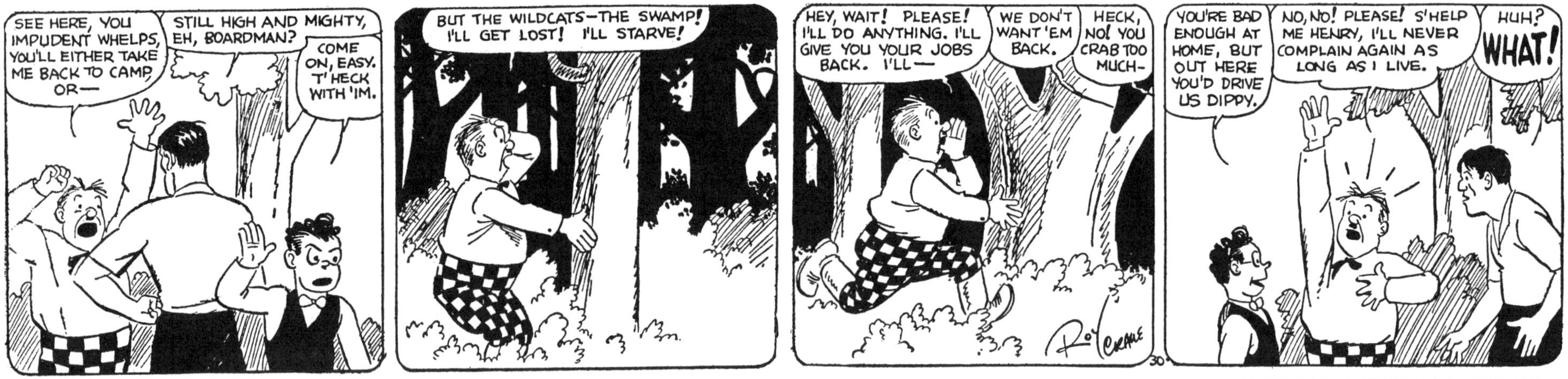

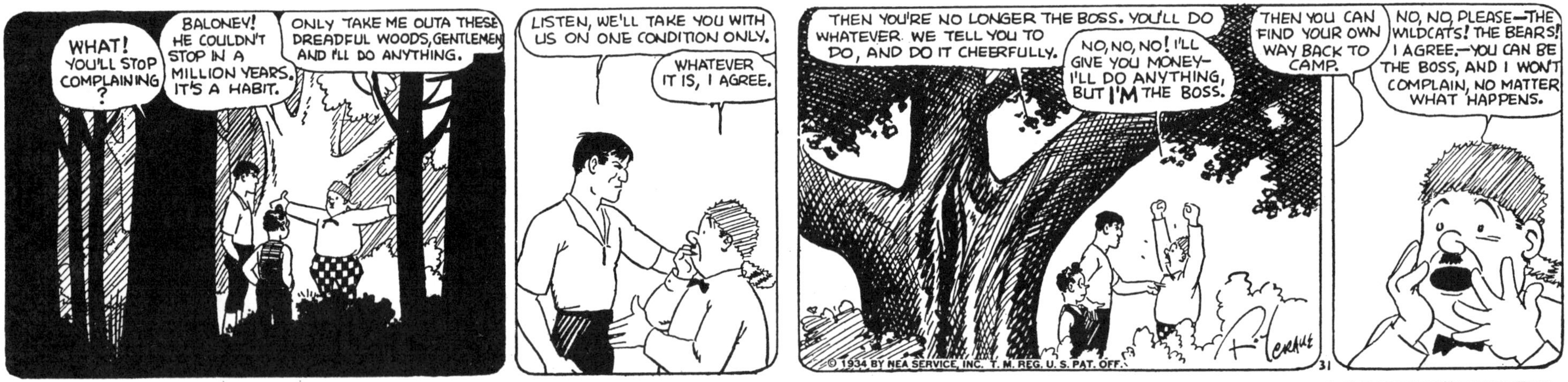

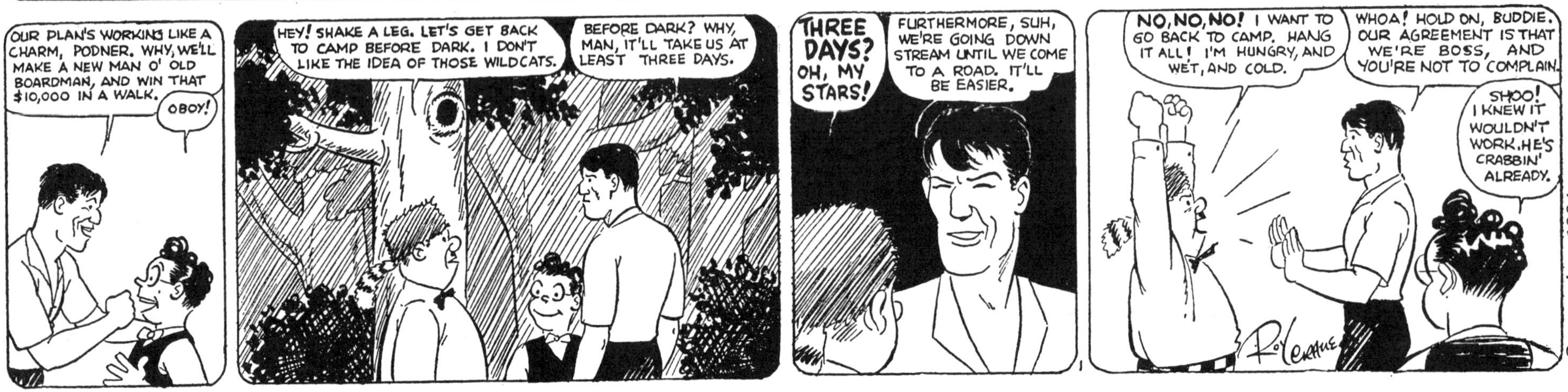

September 1934

THIS IS STUPID, IDIOTIC, INSANE! I INSIST ON GOING BACK TO CAMP!
REMEMBER, NO BEEFING.
GIVING WASH A WINK, EASY MALICIOUSLY SELECTS THE WORST POSSIBLE PATH TO FOLLOW.
OH! OWW! OUCH!
THEY CLIMB OVER ROCKS AND LOGS, AND PUSH THEIR WAY THRU DENSE THICKETS.
BUT, NO MATTER HOW TIRED, BRUISED, OR BREATHLESS, HE IS, HORATIO BOARDMAN NEVER LAGS FAR BEHIND.
OH, MY STARS! MY STARS!
HEY! LOOK OUT FOR TH' WILDCATS.
AT LAST, DOG TIRED AND BRUISED, THE PARTY STOPS FOR THE NIGHT.
IF YOU'RE STILL AFRAID O' WILDCATS, SUH, YOU CAN SLEEP IN A TREE.
ER-AH- AREN'T WE GOING TO EAT?
EAT WOT?
OW!
WITH A GROAN OF MISERY, HORATIO BOARDMAN REMEMBERS THE ELABORATE SEVEN-COURSE DINNER HE DISDAINED BACK AT HIS LODGE.
HOWEVER, THAT, NOR THE FOND RECOLLECTION OF HIS EXPENSIVE BED, NOR THE TERRIFYING THOUGHT OF WILDCATS, CAN KEEP HIM AWAKE.
© 1934 BY NEA SERVICE, INC.
T. M. REG. U. S. PAT. OFF.
GEE! YOU WERE PLENTY HARD ON TH' OLD BOY, EASY.
SURE, AND I'VE JUST STARTED. IF WE'RE GOING TO WIN THAT $10,000, PODNER, WE GOT TO BE HARD.
MORNING. HORATIO BOARDMAN WAKES WITH A START, WONDERING HOW ON EARTH HE EVER MANAGED TO SLEEP IN A TREE.
MY STARS!
OW, OW! MY LEGS, MY ARMS! EVERY MUSCLE IN MY BODY IS SORE.
TAKE A BATH IN TH' CREEK, AN' YOU'LL FEEL BETTER.
HUNGRY?
I'M STARVED, FAMISHED! OH, MY STARS! I WAS NEVER SO MISERABLE.
CHEER UP. EASY'LL SOON HAVE BREAKFAST READY.
BREAKFAST?
!
SURE. FRESH 'POSSUM. WASH CAUGHT 'IM, AND I BUILT A FIRE, BY RUBBING STICKS.

CAPTAIN EASY
by ROY CRANE
SOLDIER OF FORTUNE

CAPTAIN EASY
SOLDIER OF FORTUNE
by ROY CRANE
November 1933
THE ILL-GUARDED CARAVAN, BEARING THE MOGUL'S RANSOM, FALLS AN EASY PREY TO THE UNEXPECTED BANDIT ATTACK.
THE FABULOUS TREASURE OF $16,000,000, IS HASTILY TRANSFERRED TO DONKEYS, AND THE LOOTED CARAVAN RETURNS TO THE CITY, EMPTY-HANDED.
THE OUTLAW CHIEF IS OVERJOYED WITH HIS FOUL TREACHERY.
YAH! YAH! WE WILL PRETEND THAT WE HAVE RECEIVED NOTHING, AND FORCE THEM TO SEND ANOTHER RANSOM FOR THE ACCURSED MOGUL. YAH! YAH! YAH!
BEGONE, O UNCOMELY WENCHES, AND NEVER DARKEN MY PRINCELY YURT AGAIN.
HIS HAREM IS KICKED OUT TO MAKE ROOM FOR THE MORE ALLURING DANCING GIRLS.
A PECK OF JEWELS AND TWO BUCKETS OF GOLD TO EACH AND EVERY MAN.
THE LOOT IS DIVIDED, AND KEGS OF RICE WINE BURST OPEN.

THEN BEGINS THE BANDIT CELEBRATION, WILD, RECKLESS, BARBARIC! A CARNIVAL OF RIOTOUS JOY! MILLIONS ARE GAMBLED AWAY IN A SINGLE NIGHT, AND THERE ARE FIGHTS BY THE DOZENS.
DISGUSTED, EASY SLIPS AWAY.
PSST! YOU THINK YOUR PEOPLE WILL KICK IN WITH ANOTHER RANSOM, MOGUL?
IT IS THE FIRM OPINION OF THIS WRETCHED CAPTIVE THAT SUCH IS AN UTTER IMPOSSIBILITY, FOR THERE CANNOT BE AN OUNCE OF GOLD LEFT IN ALL MY IMPOVERISHED LAND.
JUST WHAT I THOUGHT. I'VE BROUGHT A FILE AND SOME SWORDS. I'M GOING TO HELP YOU ESCAPE.
?
11-26
QUICK- I HAVE SOME HOSSES SADDLED AND WAITING.
THE UGLY CROAKING OF MY MISERABLE THROAT CAN NEVER TRULY RECORD THE APPRECIATION OF MY SINGING HEART.
THE WILD REVELRY COMES TO A SUDDEN END
ROY CRANE
THE MOGUL'S ABSENCE IS NOTICED, AND A HUGE DRUM BOOMS A WARNING FOR ALL BANDIT OUTPOSTS TO BE ON GUARD.
NEXT WEEK: RUNNING THE GANTLET!
CAPTAIN EASY by ROY CRANE
SOLDIER OF FORTUNE

CAPTAIN EASY
SOLDIER OF FORTUNE
by ROY CRANE
December 1933

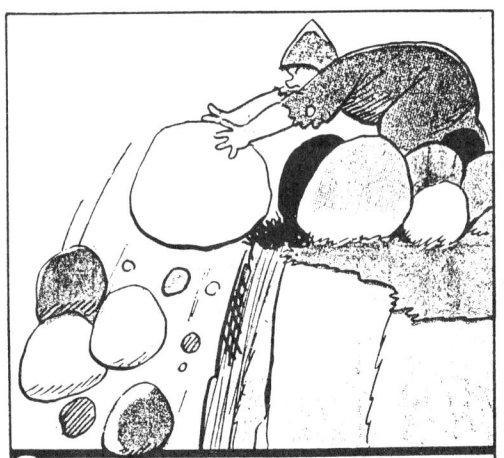

Panel 1: Booming drums sound a warning that the Mogul has escaped. From the topmost rim of the canyon, tons of boulders are hurled at the fleeing fugitives.

Panel 2: Easy's horse is killed at the start.

Panel 3: The American climbs behind the Mogul, and they ride like mad until frontier guards block their path.
"Quick, turn around! We'll try another canyon."

Panel 4: Again they race thru the hail of falling stones, miraculously escaping death, only to run into the main body of pursuing outlaws.
"Alas! Every avenue of escape is closed."

Panel 5: "We are doomed."
"Like blazes! Into this cave."

Panel 6: "Now roll this boulder into place — that'll hold 'em awhile. We got to beat 'em to the other exit."

110

111

CAPTAIN EASY
SOLDIER OF FORTUNE
by ROY CRANE
THE PINK-BEARDED PROPHET BE PRAISED! YOU ARE ALIVE.
SURE! YOU CAN'T KILL AN OLD RAWHIDE DONKEY LIKE ME, SUH.
FORTUNATELY, THE FALL ONLY KNOCKS THE BREATH OUT OF EASY.
DEATH TO THE MOGUL!
DEATH TO THE FOREIGN SWINE WHO BETRAYED US.
FROM HIGH ABOVE CAN BE HEARD THE ECHOING SHOUTS OF THE PURSUING OUTLAWS.
HASTEN, O BENEVOLENT ONE. OUR MERCILESS ENEMIES ARE ALMOST UPON US.
BUT THIS ISN'T THE WAY.
LET NO RICE GROW UNDER OUR ADVANCING FOOTSTEPS. THERE'S NO TIME TO TURN BACK.
THERE'S NO TIME TO WASTE, GETTING LOST, EITHER.
PATIENCE, O UNOBSERVANT ONE. A FAINT PATHWAY HAS ATTRACTED THE EAGLE EYES OF THIS EVER-WATCHFUL PERSON.
THEY HURRY THRU NARROW PASSAGES AND HUGE, ECHOING CAVERNS, PAST SUBTERRANEAN WATERFALLS, AND RIVERS, AND ICE COLD LAKES.

INTO A CHAMBER OF HORRORS THEY GO— A MUSTY, ROOSTING PLACE OF COUNTLESS SQUEAKING BATS— A SPOOKY PLACE FILLED WITH CHESTS AND HUMAN SKULLS.
WOW! GIVES A FELLA THE CREEPS, DOESN'T IT?
IT IS MY EARNEST DESIRE TO DEPART WITH UNBECOMING HASTE.
BLAZES! WHY, THERE'S GOLD AND SILVER IN THESE CHESTS.
ILL-FORTUNE CONTINUES TO ACCOMPANY OUR HEROIC EFFORTS, FOR MY WATCHFUL EYES FAIL TO LOCATE A PASSAGE BEYOND HERE.
IN MY ROCK-LIKE OPINION, WE SHALL HAVE TO RETRACE OUR WRETCHED FOOTSTEPS.
HOLD ON! I THINK I SMELL FRESH AIR COMING THRU HERE.
I'M SURE I DO. MAN ALIVE!! LOOK! THERE'S DAYLIGHT AHEAD.
PRAISES BE! THE RELENTLESS BANDITS NO LONGER CAN BE HEARD.
WE'RE SAFE! WE'RE FREE!!
12-10
ROY CRANE
© 1933 BY NEA SERVICE, INC.
NEXT WEEK: A BATTLE FOR LIFE!!
CAPTAIN EASY
SOLDIER OF FORTUNE
by ROY CRANE

CAPTAIN EASY
SOLDIER OF FORTUNE
by ROY CRANE

Startled at suddenly encountering a bear, face to face, the Mogul whips out his sword.

But before he can strike, the huge beast gives a thundering growl and knocks him galley west.

Easy, equally startled, leaps to the rescue, scoring a lightning-like thrust to the heart.

Another sweep of the bear's powerful paw and Easy's sword sails into space—he dashes into the cave with the enraged monster in hot pursuit.

Just as the American is about to be overtaken, the mortally wounded bear drops dead.

"BLAZES! WHAT A CLOSE CALL THAT WAS!"

115

CAPTAIN EASY by ROY CRANE
SOLDIER OF FORTUNE
EASY LANDS WITH A TERRIFIC SPLASH!!
DAZED, BUT STILL HOLDING THE LIMP FORM OF THE MOGUL, HE STRUGGLES TO THE SURFACE AMIDST A SHOWER OF SPEARS FROM THE INFURIATED OUTLAWS ABOVE.
!
GIVING OUT OF SPEARS, THE VILLAINOUS RASCALS HURL LOGS AND STONES AT HIM.
YAH! YAH! YAH!
BUT EASY WELCOMES THE LOGS. CLUTCHING TWO OF THEM, HE IMPROVISES A CRUDE RAFT, AND THE MOUNTAIN TORRENT QUICKLY SWEEPS HIM DOWNSTREAM.
FASTER AND FASTER HE GOES—SO FAST THAT HE PASSES ANOTHER GROUP OF BANDITS BEFORE THEY HAVE TIME TO GET OUT THEIR SPEARS.
CAPTAIN EASY by ROY CRANE
SOLDIER OF FORTUNE

117

CAPTAIN EASY
SOLDIER OF FORTUNE
by ROY CRANE
WITH EASY'S PLUNGE OVER THE WATERFALL, EVERYTHING BECOMES A BLANK. HE REMEMBERS NOTHING OF STRUGGLING TO THE SURFACE, STILL CLUTCHING THE MOGUL.
OR OF BEING HELPLESSLY CAUGHT IN A WHIRLPOOL.
HE HAS ONLY A VAGUE SENSATION OF HEARING FAR-AWAY VOICES.
AIE! THEY ARE DROWNING.
CATCH THEM BY THE HAIR. SAVE THEM!
THE NEXT THING HE KNOWS, HE IS LYING ON A COUCH IN A LUXURIOUS WHEELED TENT, AND A SLAVE GIRL IS STROKING HIS HAIR.
THE ALL POWERFUL SON OF HEAVEN ANXIOUSLY AWAITS THE RETURN OF YOUR UNBELIEVABLE STRENGTH.
?

CAPTAIN EASY

★ ★ ★

SOLDIER OF FORTUNE

WHEN the giant condors reached their nest, Easy managed to free himself, only to be seized again by the Great Mogul. Then bandits swooped in and captured both of them, and took them to a mountain hideout. A fabulous ransom was demanded for the Mogul's release. The ransom was paid, but the bandits demanded another. Then Easy escaped, taking the Mogul with him, and agreed to lead an army against the bandits, to try and recover the ransom.

HURRY!

Taking command of the Mogul's army, Easy sends for a sub-machine gun on his wrecked plane, large quantities of varnished silk and some light rope.

The silk he orders sewed together to form a huge, hollow ball, which he encloses in a network of rope.

While the Mogul and all his men look on, mystified, he inflates the ball with hot air from a small fire.

Then, his balloon ready and the wind just right, Easy takes off! 500, 1000, 1500 feet he soars, while the army below gasps in amazement.

As the hot air begins to cool, down he comes, barely reaching the edge of the towering precipice.

Immediately a dozen blood-thirsty outlaws rush toward him with swords and spears.

CAPTAIN EASY by ROY CRANE
SOLDIER OF FORTUNE

January 1934

CAPTAIN EASY
★ ★ ★
SOLDIER OF FORTUNE

120

121

NO PARADE OF A CAESAR THRU THE STREETS OF ANCIENT ROME EVER SURPASSED THE TRIUMPHANT RETURN OF THE GREAT MOGUL, AT THE HEAD OF HIS CONQUERING ARMY.
WOMEN TEAR THEIR HAIR IN A FRENZY OF DELIGHT. SILKEN ROBES ARE THROWN IN THE WARRIOR'S PATH. TRUMPETS BLARE. FIRECRACKERS BOOM. THE DIN IS FRIGHTFUL.
POW!
UM
PAH!
EASY, HERO OF THE HOUR, IS DECORATED BEFORE THE MULTITUDE.
AND, IN TOKEN OF THE MONARCH'S APPRECIATION, IS GIVEN A MAGNIFICENT HOME.
YOURS, O-HONORED FOREIGNER
FOURTEEN TREASURE CHESTS, LADEN WITH GOLD AND SILVER AND PRECIOUS GEMS ARE BROUGHT.
HIS STABLES ARE FILLED WITH FINE CAMELS AND ELEPHANTS AND HORSES.
CAPTAIN EASY
SOLDIER OF FORTUNE

123

CAPTAIN EASY
SOLDIER OF FORTUNE
by ROY CRANE
YOU LOOK SICK, BUDDIE.
THESE WRETCHED LIPS HAVE NOT TOUCHED WATER IN TWO DAYS.
BORED WITH BEING RICH AND RIDING ON GAYLY DECORATED ELEPHANTS, EASY MINGLES WITH THE COMMON PEOPLE, AND IS TOUCHED WITH THEIR SUFFERING.
WHY DON'T YOU GO TO THE LAKE?
IT IS WRITTEN IN THE BOOKS OF LAW, O WELL-MEANING ONE, THAT THE LAKE IS MEANT FOR SHIPS TO SAIL UPON, AND NOT FOR DRINKING.
THEN GO TO THE PUBLIC WELL.
ALAS! I AM A POOR MAN WITHOUT COINS OF COPPER.
YOU MEAN IT COSTS MONEY FOR EVEN A SINGLE DRINK?
AIE! THE WELLS ARE OWNED BY FAVORITES OF THE MOGUL, WHO GROW EXCEEDINGLY RICH BY EXPLOITING THE PUBLIC.
BLAZES! NO WONDER THESE BOZOS ARE DIRTY.
EASY HASTENS TO THE ROYAL PALACE.

125

CAPTAIN EASY by ROY CRANE
SOLDIER OF FORTUNE
WHAT'S GOING ON, BUDDIE?
A PIRATE SHIP IS IN PORT.
AIE! THEY ARE BRINGING SLAVES TO THE MARKET. THERE WILL BE RARE BARGAINS.
WHO WILL GIVE A BUCKET OF SILVER FOR THIS STOUT FEMALE?
NAY! SHE EATS TOO MUCH.
HALF A BUCKET.
EASY STANDS AGHAST, WATCHING MEN AND WOMEN BEING AUCTIONED OFF LIKE SO MANY SHEEP.
SOLD FOR HALF A BUCKET OF SILVER.
BUT WHY ARE THEY TO BECOME SLAVES?
WHY NOT? THEY ARE DONKEYS OF KASHNO, OUR HATED ENEMIES. THEY DESERVE NOTHING.
EASY CANNOT SEE THE JUSTICE OF IT. HIS HEART GOES OUT TO THESE POOR, FRIENDLESS PEOPLE..........
ESPECIALLY TO A BEAUTIFUL GIRL OF AUBURN HAIR, WHO WEEPS CONSTANTLY.
BY THE DYE OF HER HAIR SHE IS THE DAUGHTER OF AN EMIR.
AIE! SEE HOW PROUDLY SHE HOLDS HER SHAPELY HEAD.
YAH, YAH! BUT SHE WILL NOT BE PROUD FOR LONG.

127

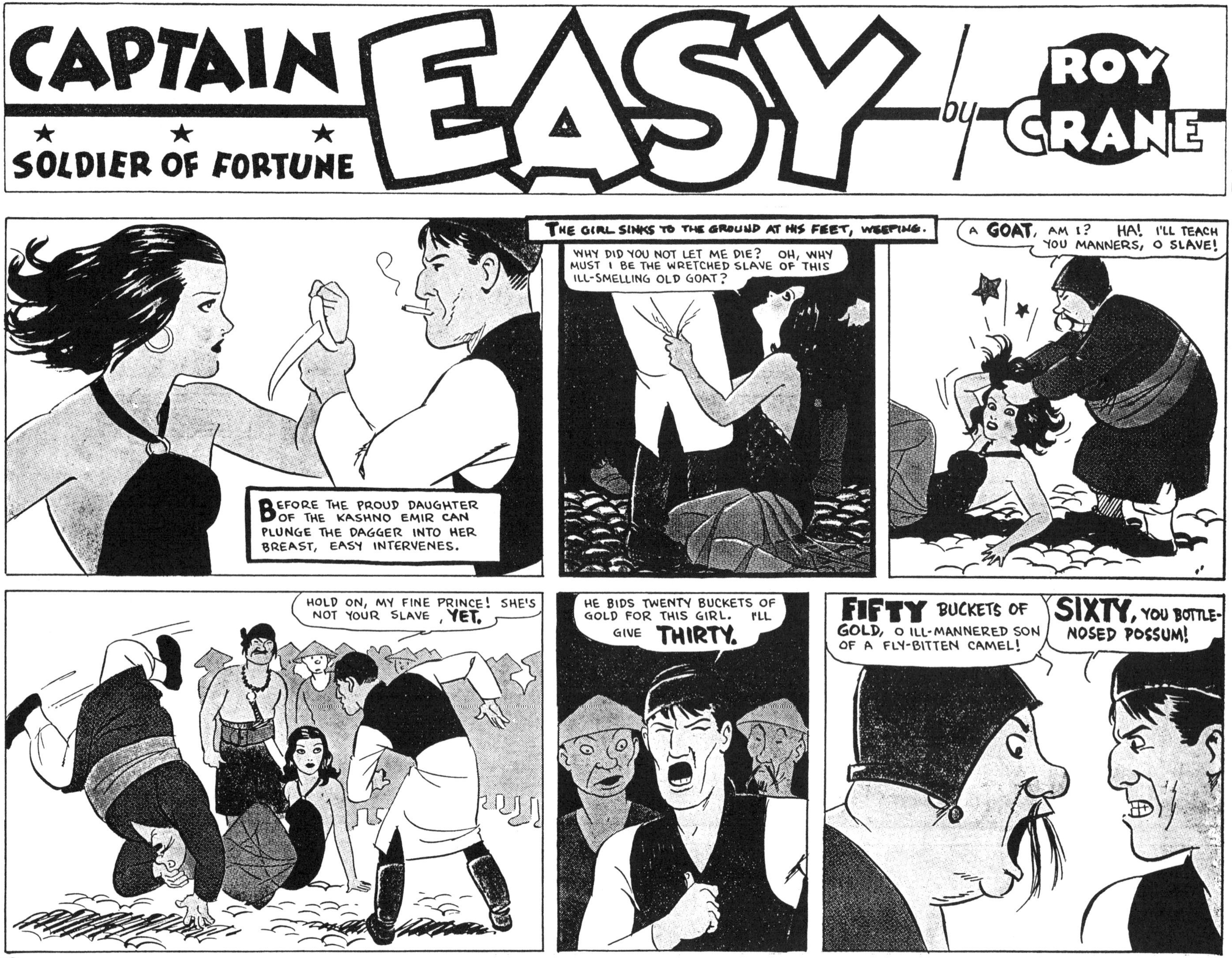

February 1934

ONE HUNDRED!
HUNDRED AND TEN!
THE BEAUTIFUL REDHEAD SMILES THRU HER TEARS AT EASY. THE PIRATE IS OVERJOYED. PRINCE WOBY GONG SCREAMS IN RAGE.
ONE HUNDRED AND --- URK!!
ANOTHER BID, BLAST YOU, AND I'LL RIP YOU OPEN.
EE-YI! SOLD TO THE FINE FOREIGNER FOR 110 BUCKETS OF GLITTERING GOLD!
SHYLY, THE DAUGHTER OF THE EMIR TRIES TO EXPRESS HER GRATITUDE.
MY LIFE IS YOURS, O KINDLY MASTER. COMMAND WHAT YOU WILL, AND ROSE PETAL WILL SMILINGLY OBEY.
AW, FORGET IT, MA'M. HERE — YOU'RE FREE — TAKE THIS MONEY AND GO HOME TO YOUR PEOPLE.
THE GIRL STARES IN AMAZEMENT AS EASY RIDES OFF.
HI HO! BROKE AGAIN. I'M A BLINKING OLD FOOL, I RECKON, BUT I COULDN'T HELP FEELING SORRY FOR THE POOR KID.
WHAT! YOU HERE?
ROSE PETAL IS YOUR SLAVE. SHE HAS NO HOME BUT YOUR HOME. WHEREVER YOU GO, O KINDLY ONE, ROSE PETAL WILL FOLLOW.
NEXT WEEK: AN ENEMY.
CAPTAIN EASY
SOLDIER OF FORTUNE
by ROY CRANE

CAPTAIN EASY by ROY CRANE
SOLDIER OF FORTUNE
NOT KNOWING WHAT ELSE TO DO, EASY BIDS THE SLAVE GIRL ENTER. SHYLY, SHE LOOKS OVER HER NEW HOME.
WHY ARE YOU KEEPING A DOG? ARE YOU GOING TO EAT HIM?
BLAZES, NO! DO YOUR PEOPLE EAT DOGS?
NAY, O KINDLY MASTER, BUT MY SCHOLARLY UNCLE, WHO HAS TRAVELED FAR, SAYS THAT FOREIGNERS ARE FOOLS WHO WILL DO ANYTHING.
YOU TELL YOUR UNCLE HE'S COO-COO.
MY LEARNED UNCLE IS DEAD, O KINDLY ONE. WE DROWNED HIM LAST SPRING.
YOU WHAT?
DROWNED HIM. HO LA! DO NOT THE PEOPLE OF YOUR LAND DROWN THEIR PARENTS WHEN THEY GROW TOO OLD TO WORK?
BLAZES, NO! WE'RE KIND TO 'EM—WE KEEP 'EM.
AIE! IT IS A MOST UNUSUAL CUSTOM. WE SOMETIMES KEEP CATS AS PETS, BUT NEVER AGED PARENTS.
CAPTAIN EASY by ROY CRANE
SOLDIER OF FORTUNE

CAPTAIN EASY
★ ★ ★ SOLDIER OF FORTUNE

Panel 1: ONCE IT WAS AGREED TO KEEP AN OLD PHILOSOPHER OF MY LAND AS A PET, BUT, ALAS, IT WAS UNSUCCESSFUL. HE WOULD NOT LIVE ON MICE.
— THAT'S A HOT ONE.

Panel 2: NOW WHAT? / IS IT NOT THE CUSTOM, O HEAVENLY ONE, FOR A SLAVE TO BATHE THE HANDS AND FEET OF THE MASTER BEFORE EACH MEAL?

Panel 3: AW, NIX. I DON'T EAT WITH MY TOES. BESIDES, ROSE PETAL, YOU'RE FREE. I WON'T HAVE YOU FOR A SLAVE. UNDERSTAND?

Panel 4: IF I DISPLEASE YOU, O LIGHT OF MY LIFE, SLAY ME, BURN ME, CAST MY WRETCHED BODY TO THE DOGS, FOR THE TINKLING BELLS WILL HAVE LEFT MY SINGING HEART.

Panel 5: CAN'T YOU UNDERSTAND? I JUST DON'T BELIEVE IN SLAVERY. I LIKE YOU, ROSE PETAL. I WANT TO HELP YOU. AND, IN A FEW DAYS, I'M GOING TO TAKE YOU HOME TO YOUR PEOPLE.

Panel 6: MEANWHILE, PRINCE WOBY GONG HASTENS TO THE GREAT MOGUL. / AIE! A BEAUTIFUL SLAVE GIRL, AND THAT DOG OF A FOREIGNER SNATCHED HER FROM MY VERY GRASP. / PATIENCE, O OVERWROUGHT UNCLE, AND THIS GIFTED MONARCH WILL FIND A WAY TO REGAIN HER.

NEXT WEEK: THE MOGUL'S SISTER.

2-11 © 1934

CAPTAIN EASY
SOLDIER OF FORTUNE
by ROY CRANE
EASY IS ATTRACTED BY THE BLARING OF A HORN AT HIS DOOR.
YOU SELLING FISH?
NAY, O MOST FORTUNATE OF MEN. AS A MESSENGER OF THE GREAT MOGUL, I BRING GLAD NEWS.
IN TOKEN OF HIS HIGH ESTEEM FOR YOU, THE SUPREME SON OF HEAVEN GRACIOUSLY OFFERS HIS FAVORITE SISTER IN HOLY WEDLOCK.
?
THE DOOR OF THE LITTER OPENS, AND OUT TUMBLES THE BLUSHING BRIDE-TO-BE, PRINCESS WOTTA TA MATA.
STEADY, O HEAVEN-BORN! STEADY.
!!
WHAT!!! ME MARRY THAT OLD MOTH-EATEN HIPPOPOTAMUS?
HAVE A CARE, O TACTLESS COMMONER. THE MOGUL IS ALL POWERFUL. TO SPURN SUCH A MAGNIFICENT HONOR WOULD BE AN INSULT TO THE ROYAL FAMILY.
CAPTAIN EASY
SOLDIER OF FORTUNE

133

CAPTAIN EASY
SOLDIER OF FORTUNE
by ROY CRANE
WHAT! THAT DOG OF A FOREIGNER REFUSES TO WED MY WELL-FATTENED SISTER?
AIE, O HEAVEN-BORN. HE FLEES TOWARD THE LAND OF THE DESPISED KASHNOS WITH THE FORBIDDEN SLAVE GIRL.
INGRATE! BROTHER OF A WART! SON OF A SWINE WHICH WALLOWS IN GARBAGE HEAPS! HOW DARE HE DEFY ME! HOW DARE HE INSULT MY HONORED FAMILY!
THE MOGUL IS ENRAGED!
BUM BIDDY BUM!
PRESENTLY, FROM THE HIGHEST CASTLE TOWER, THERE BOOMS A GIGANTIC DRUM.
ITS STRANGE RHYTHMIC BEAT IS HEARD BY A GROUP OF WARRIORS TEN MILES AWAY.
BUM BIDDY BUM!
BUM BIDDY BUM!
WHAT DOES IT SAY, O BEATER OF TOM-TOMS?
AH YAH! THE WAR-LIKE FOREIGN DEVIL IS A TRAITOR. HE APPROACHES WITH HASTENING FOOTSTEPS, AND IS TO BE CAPTURED DEAD OR ALIVE.
BUM BIDDY BUM!
BUM! BIDDY BUM!
THE WAR PARTY RELAYS THE MESSAGE.

135

CAPTAIN EASY
SOLDIER OF FORTUNE
by ROY CRANE
March 1934
ROSE PETAL BEGINS TO WEEP.
ALAS, O LIGHT OF THE MOON, THE GODS OF MERCY FROWN UPON OUR FRUITLESS EFFORTS TO ESCAPE. NO MATTER WHICH WAY WE TURN, THE RELENTLESS WARRIORS OF THE ANGERED MOGUL ARE BEFORE US.
EASY SAYS NOTHING, BUT BEADS OF SWEAT APPEAR ON HIS BROW, AS THE MADDENING, RHYTHMIC THROB OF THE WAR DRUMS GROWS LOUDER AND NEARER.
DIBBY DABBY DUM DUM!
WE GOT TO GET OUT O' THIS. HEAD FOR THE LAKE. STOP FOR NOTHING!
DIBBY DABBY DUM DUM!
THE DRUM BEATS SUDDENLY STOP. THERE IS NO SOUND EXCEPT FOR THE ELEPHANT CRASHING THRU THE BRUSH.
THEN A BLOOD-CURDLING WAR WHOOP, AS HALF A HUNDRED MEN LEAP INTO THE OPEN, HURLING DARTS AND SPEARS.

THE LOYAL MAHOUT FALLS TO THE GROUND, DEAD. THE ELEPHANT SQUEALS IN PAIN. THE TOP OF THE HOWDAH IS KNOCKED GALLEY-WEST BY AN OVERHANGING LIMB.
HI YI! WE MADE IT!
NAY, NAY, LISTEN! THE DRUMS CAN BE HEARD AGAIN. THERE IS STILL ANOTHER CIRCLE OF WARRIORS BEFORE US.
JUMPING BLUE BLAZES! YOU'RE RIGHT. QUICK! GRAB HOLD O' MY NECK.
DIBBY DABBY DUM DUM!
ATTA GIRL! HOLD ON FOR DEAR LIFE.
WHAT LUCK! I DROPPED MY SUB-MACHINE GUN.
ILL-FORTUNE FALLS UPON US LIKE RAIN FROM THE UPPER AIR. WE DARE NOT DESCEND; AND THE MERCILESS WARRIORS HAVE BUT TO GLANCE HEAVENWARD TO DISCOVER OUR ILL-CONCEALED REFUGE.
DIBBY DABBY DUM DUM!
DIBBY DABBY DUM DUM!
NEXT WEEK: LIBERTY OR DEATH.
3-4 © 1934 BY NEA SERVICE, INC.
ROY CRANE
CAPTAIN EASY
SOLDIER OF FORTUNE
by ROY CRANE

WHILE TOM-TOMS THROB AND A THOUSAND WARRIORS COMB THE WOODS FOR HIM, EASY TRIES TO PLAN A MEANS OF ESCAPE.
!
BEFORE HE CAN EVOLVE A SUITABLE PLAN, THO, TWO WARRIORS FIND HIS SUB-MACHINE GUN BENEATH THE VERY TREE WHERE HE AND ROSE PETAL ARE HIDING.
THEY ARE ABOUT TO SOUND THE ALARM WHICH SURELY WOULD LEAD TO HIS DISCOVERY WHEN...
BLAZES! NOW OR NEVER!
?
KNOCKED 'EM COLD. QUICK— GET INTO THIS FELLA'S PETTICOAT.
IT IS ILL-FITTING, O LIGHT OF MY LIFE. IT IS MOST UNBECOMING.
WELL, THERE'S NO TIME TO CALL A TAILOR. I'VE GOT TO HIDE THESE BOZOS AND RUN.
CAPTAIN EASY SOLDIER OF FORTUNE by ROY CRANE
CAPTAIN EASY SOLDIER of FORTUNE by ROY CRANE

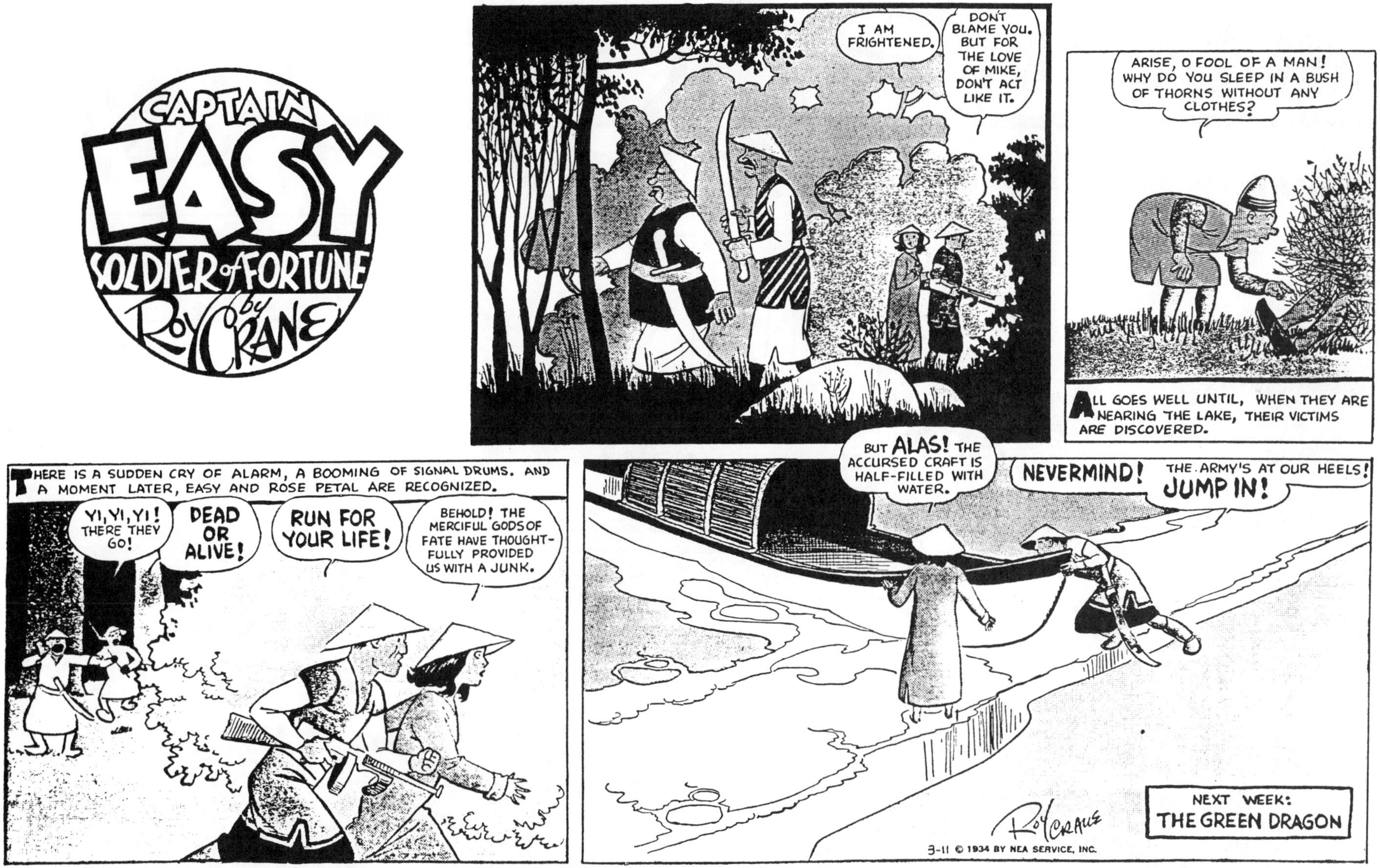

Laugh With the Best Comics Daily in The News

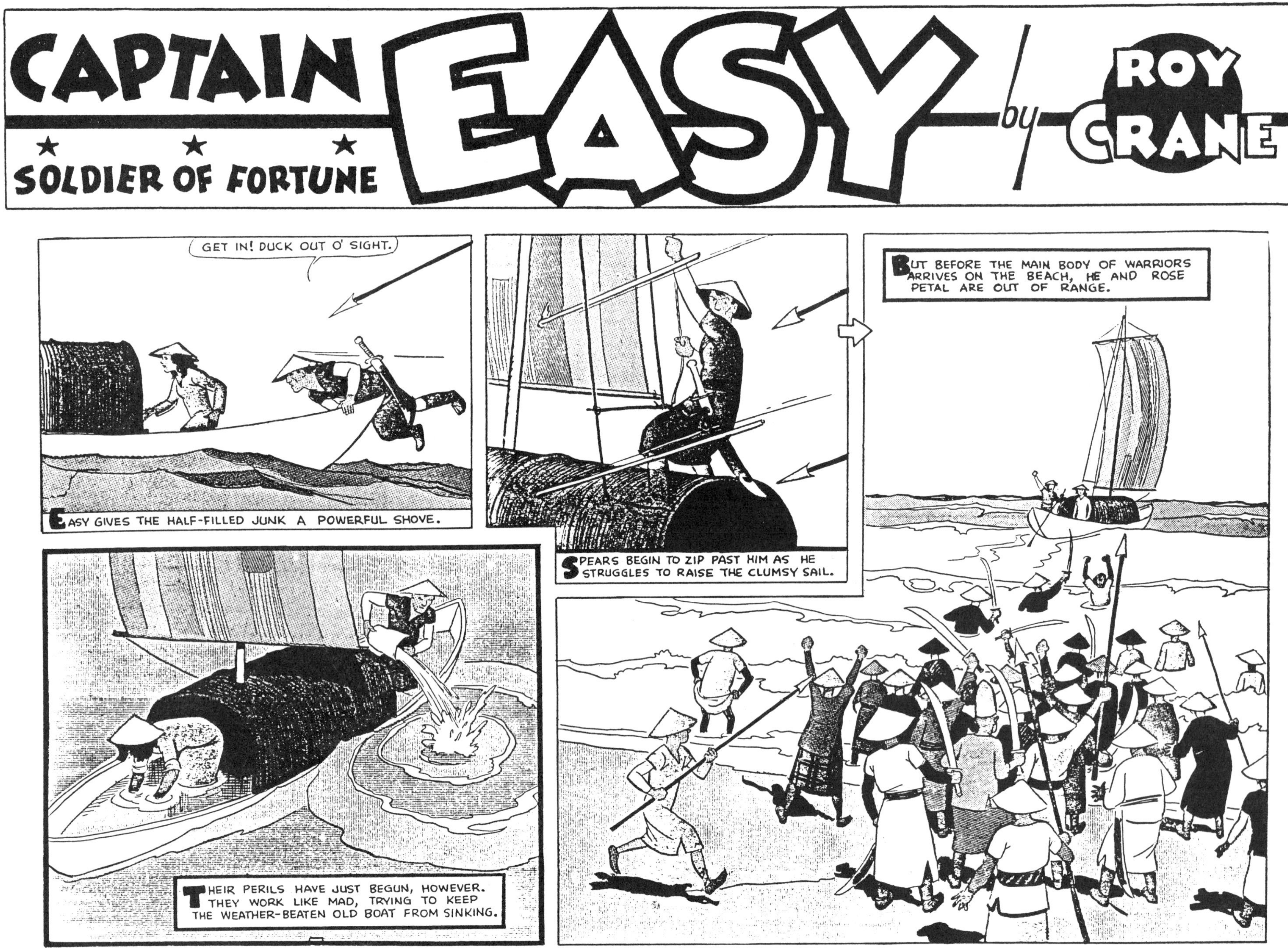
CAPTAIN EASY
SOLDIER OF FORTUNE
by ROY CRANE
GET IN! DUCK OUT O' SIGHT.
EASY GIVES THE HALF-FILLED JUNK A POWERFUL SHOVE.
SPEARS BEGIN TO ZIP PAST HIM AS HE STRUGGLES TO RAISE THE CLUMSY SAIL.
BUT BEFORE THE MAIN BODY OF WARRIORS ARRIVES ON THE BEACH, HE AND ROSE PETAL ARE OUT OF RANGE.
THEIR PERILS HAVE JUST BEGUN, HOWEVER. THEY WORK LIKE MAD, TRYING TO KEEP THE WEATHER-BEATEN OLD BOAT FROM SINKING.

Laugh With the Best Comics Daily in The News

CAPTAIN EASY by ROY CRANE
SOLDIER OF FORTUNE
BLAZES! THIS IS WORSE THAN THE MOGUL'S ARMY.
ALAS! THE LUCKLESS MICE HAVE LEAPED FROM THE TRAP INTO THE RELENTLESS JAWS OF THE CAT.
THE FLEET PIRATE JUNK IS GAINING RAPIDLY!!
BUM!
AND OPENS FIRE WITH A PRIMITIVE, WOODEN CANNON.
?
PLUNK!
YA YA YAH!
THE VILLAINOUS RUFFIANS HOWL WITH DELIGHT-
!
WOP!
AND SEND ANOTHER SHOT CRASHING THRU THE SAIL.

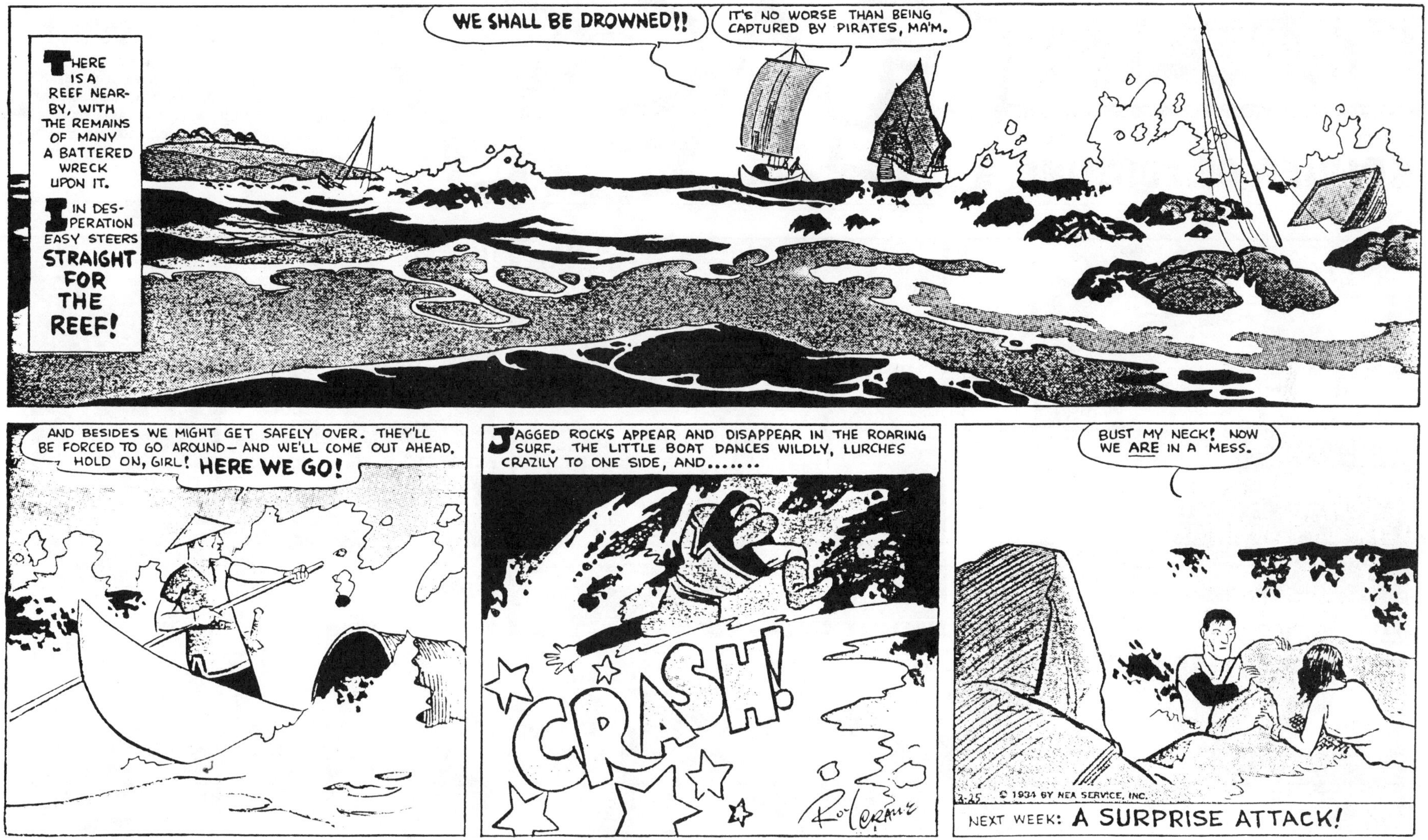

Laugh With the Best Comics Daily in The News

144

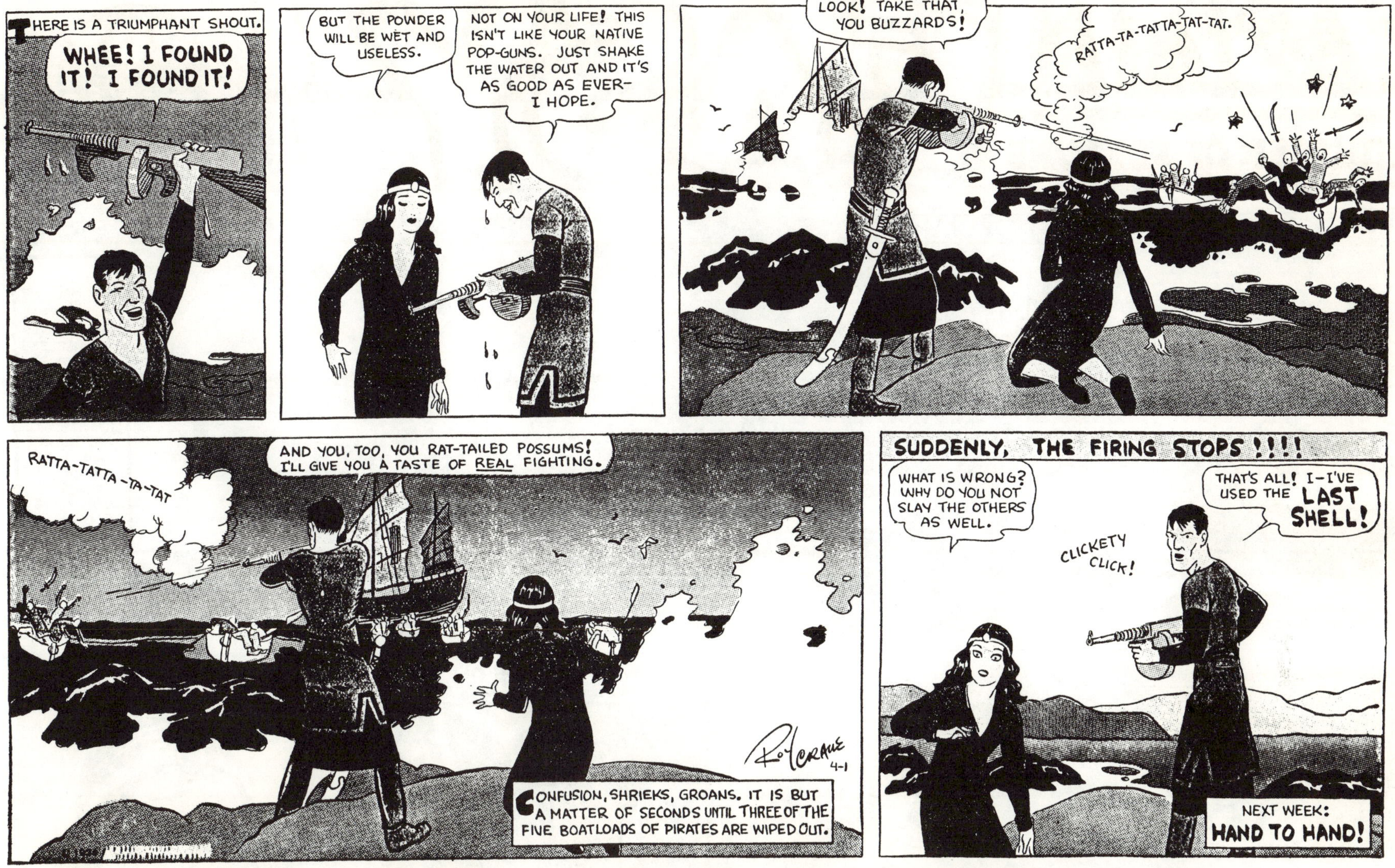

CAPTAIN EASY
★ ★ ★ SOLDIER OF FORTUNE

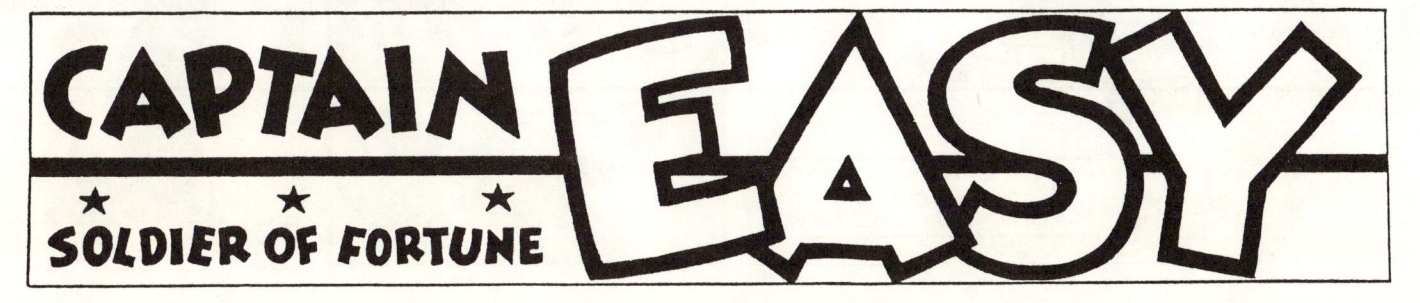

CAPTAIN EASY
SOLDIER OF FORTUNE
REG. U. S. PAT. OFF.
by ROY CRANE
OW!
LOOKOUT!
PLOP!
HIS MACHINE GUN EMPTY, EASY HURLS THE USELESS WEAPON AT THE NEAREST PIRATES. HE THROWS WITH ALL HIS MIGHT, AND THE RASCALS, TRYING TO DODGE THE BLOW, SUCCEED ONLY IN OVERTURNING THE BOAT.
YOU'LL NEVER TAKE ME ALIVE, YOU THIEVING RATS!
WHIPPING OUT HIS SWORD, THE PLUCKY AMERICAN TRIES TO FIGHT BACK THE OTHER CREW.
BUT HIS FOOT SLIPS ON THE MOSSY ROCK.
ROSE PETAL SCREAMS, BELIEVING THAT THE END HAS COME.

147

CAPTAIN EASY
SOLDIER OF FORTUNE
by ROY CRANE
BLAZES! I THOUGHT YOU SAID YOU WERE TOUGH.
MIXING JIU JITSU WITH HARD RIGHTS AND LEFTS, EASY QUICKLY SUBDUES HANG HI, THE VILLAINOUS PIRATE CHIEF.
AND, TO ROSE PETAL'S SURPRISE, PICKS HIM UP AND THROWS HIM OVER HIS SHOULDER.
SURELY, YOU--YOU'RE NOT BRINGING HIM ALONG?
SURE. HE'S GOING TO BRING GOOD LUCK.
NAY, NAY! BEHEAD HIM! DROWN HIM! IT IS WRITTEN THAT THE WISE MAN TRAMPLES THE SCORPION THAT WOULD STING HIM.
ON THE OTHER HAND, ONLY A SAP WOULD KILL A GOOSE THAT LAYS GOLDEN EGGS.
GOLDEN EGGS?
SURE. HE'S PROTECTION. TELL YOUR CUT-THROAT CREW, HANG HI, WHAT'LL HAPPEN IF THEY THROW EVEN A SINGLE SPEAR AT US.
?
TELL 'EM, BLAST YOU!
STAND OFF, OR THE ACCURSED SWINE WILL RIP ME OPEN.

ATTABOY! NOW GET BUSY WITH THOSE OARS. YOU SEE, ROSE PETAL, HE'S PROTECTING US AND SAVING US SOME LABOR, AS WELL. WHAT'S MORE, HE'S GOING TO BRING US A PILE O' MONEY.
HOW?
WELL, HE'S THE VERY PIRATE WHO CAPTURED AND SOLD YOU. WE'LL PLAY HIS OWN GAME, AND SELL HIM.
AYE. MY HONORED FATHER WOULD GLADLY GIVE A SACK OF GOLD FOR THE PRIVILEGE OF CUTTING OFF HIS EVIL HEAD.
NIX! AN EYE FOR AN EYE. WE'LL SELL HIM BACK TO HIMSELF. HE HAS A FORTUNE, IN GOLD THAT I PAID FOR YOUR FREEDOM, AND I AIM TO GET IT BACK.
FOOL OF A MAN IN A WOMAN'S PETTICOAT! O COUSIN OF A CAMEL'S BREATH! O BROTHER OF A TURNIP, CURSES UPON YOU! MAY I LIVE TO SEE THE DAY WHEN YOU'RE AT MY MERCY.
SIT DOWN, YOU PIG-FACED POSSUM! I MAY DECIDE TO SELL YOU TO THE GIRL'S FATHER, AFTER ALL.
HANG HI PROTESTS, CURSES AND THREATENS IN VAIN.
YOU ARE RICH!
THE PROBLEM, NOW, IS WHAT TO DO WITH THE BLASTED STUFF.
WITHIN TWO DAYS THE ARRANGEMENTS ARE COMPLETED, AND HE IS FORCED TO GIVE UP THE ILL-GAINED FORTUNE, IN ORDER TO SAVE HIS HEAD.
NEXT WEEK: THE DONKEY MAN.
© 1934
4-15
Roy Crane
CAPTAIN EASY
SOLDIER OF FORTUNE

CAPTAIN EASY
SOLDIER OF FORTUNE
by ROY CRANE
O MASTER, ISN'T IT GORGEOUS?
I RECKON SO, BUT WHAT THE BLAZES AM I GOING TO DO, IN THE DESERT, WITH THE CHESTS OF GOLD?
ROSE PETAL WEEPS WITH JOY AT THE SIGHT OF HER BELOVED HOMELAND.
AT HER INSISTENCE EASY BURIES HIS GOLD IN THE SAND.
WHAT'S THE IDEA? BANDITS?
AIE! IN KASHNO ONE MUST HIDE EVEN HIS SHADOW.
TEAR YOUR CLOTHES, TOO. AND SMEAR DIRT ON THEM. IT IS NOT SAFE TO APPEAR PROSPEROUS WHEN TRAVELING.
THANKS. THIS COUNTRY'S FULL O' QUAINT CUSTOMS, ISN'T IT?
AND ANOTHER THING- IF PURCHASING ONLY A PIN, IT IS WISE TO HAGGLE OVER THE PRICE, OR SOMEONE MAY THINK YOU ARE RICH AND TRY TO CUT YOUR THROAT.
NICE PEOPLE.
AIE, YOU WILL LOVE MY COUNTRY, O MIGHTY ONE. IT IS A MAN'S PARADISE. SELDOM DOES A DAY PASS WITHOUT THREE OR FOUR FIGHTS.

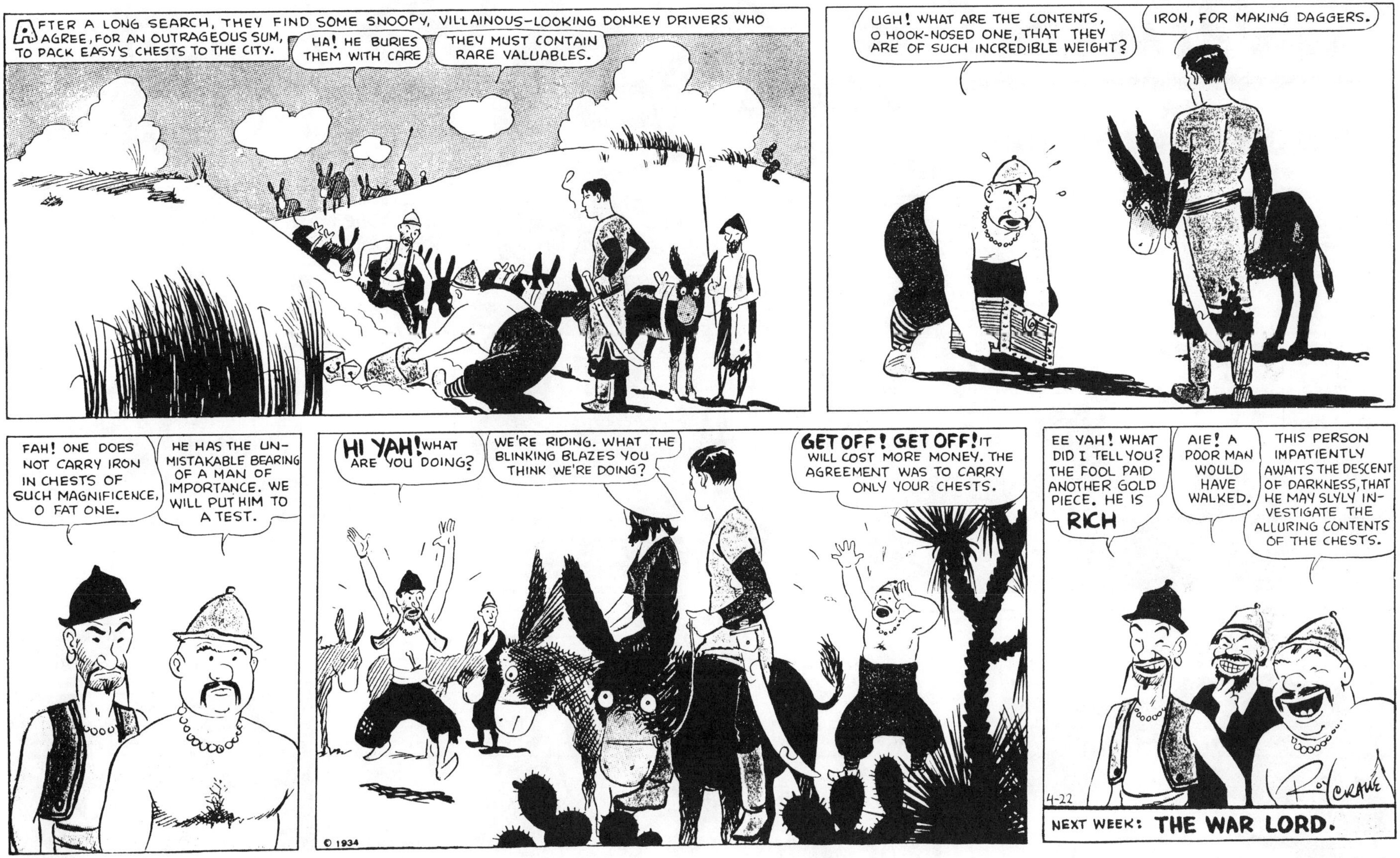

Laugh With the Best Comics Daily in The News

CAPTAIN EASY

SOLDIER OF FORTUNE

by ROY CRANE

Easy watches the shifty-eyed donkey drivers like a hawk, and thanks his stars they don't know what they're carrying. All goes well until the caravan is making camp for the night.

"HORSEMEN!"

"PERHAPS THEY ARE THIEVING BANDITS, IN SEARCH OF LOOT."

"THEN, GET YOUR MEN READY FOR A FIGHT."

"GET YOUR MEN READY, I SAID!"

"YOU PAID US TO CARRY YOUR CHESTS, O MERCHANT— NOT TO PROTECT THEM."

"MORE GOLD. MORE GOLD."

"BLAST YOU! YOU'RE WORSE THAN BANDITS! HOW MUCH?"

"FOR 30 PIECES OF GOLD WE FIGHT OUTLAWS HALF-HEARTEDLY, AND FOR 20 PIECES WE RUN AT THE FIRST OPPORTUNITY. BUT FOR 50 PIECES WE BATTLE LIKE DEVIL-DEMONS."

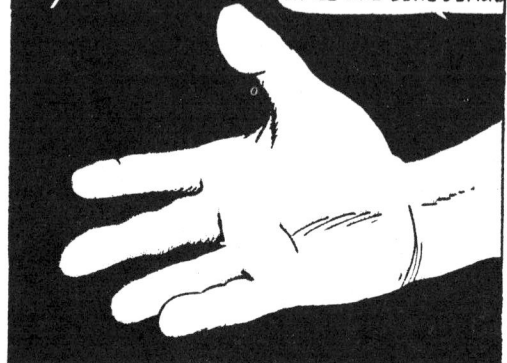

No sooner have the crafty donkey men been paid, than the horsemen are upon them.

"I AM SARDEENA KHAN, MIGHTY WAR LORD OF THE DESERT, WHO DEMANDS TRIBUTE FOR YOUR SAFE JOURNEY."

"AND WHAT IF I REFUSE?"

Then Sardeena Khan regrets his inability to induce his fatigued men to drive away three score bandits, hiding beyond yonder hill.

CAPTAIN EASY by ROY CRANE

Panel 1: "IT'S A BLINKING RACKET! A HOLD-UP! HE'S AS MUCH A BANDIT AS--" "PRAY GUARD THY TONGUE, O CARELESS ONE. IT IS THE CUSTOM TO PAY TRIBUTE." "AIE, SARDEENA KHAN IS ALL-POWERFUL." "REMEMBER, O FOOL, WE DID NOT AGREE TO FIGHT A WAR LORD."

Panel 2: While the others are trying to reason with Easy, a warrior opens one of the chests. "GOLD! GOLD!"

Panel 3: "HI YI! DID I NOT SAY HE WAS RICH?" "GOLD! MANY CHESTS OF GLITTERING GOLD!" "HI, YI, YI!" The secret is out. The donkey men stare in pop-eyed amazement, and lick their lips in greedy anticipation.

Panel 4: Then Sardeena Khan departs with a load of tribute, leaving Easy to protect the rest of his riches, as best he can.

Panel 5: One of the drivers, his eyes glittering with excitement, brings Easy's dinner. "I DON'T TRUST 'EM, ROSE PETAL. BETTER GIVE PART O' YOUR FOOD TO THE DOGS, BEFORE EATING." "?"

Panel 6: The act of caution saves Easy's life and perhaps Rose Petal's, as well, for in ten minutes the dogs are dead. "THE FOOD WAS POISONED!" "WELL, YOUNG LADY, IT LOOKS AS THO WE'RE GOING TO HAVE TO WATCH OUR STEP FOR AWHILE."

NEXT WEEK: DESERT CUNNING

© 1934 BY NEA SERVICE, INC. — Roy Crane 4-29

CAPTAIN EASY
SOLDIER OF FORTUNE
by ROY CRANE
DESPITE THE EVER-LURKING DANGER, THIS DEVOTED SLAVE FEARS SHE CANNOT REMAIN AWAKE MUCH LONGER.
SURE. THAT'S O.K., ROSE PETAL. YOU GO TO SLEEP, I'LL KEEP AN EYE ON THINGS.
ROSE PETAL AWAKENS NEXT MORNING TO FIND THE CHESTS STILL THERE, AND EASY AS WATCHFUL AS EVER.
DID THE UNTRUSTWORTHY RUFFIANS TRY TO STEAL YOUR PRECIOUS CHESTS OF GOLD?
UNEVENTFUL HOURS PASS... THEN, QUICKLY, THE DONKEY MEN STRIKE.
WHAT THE BLAZES?
BEFORE ROSE PETAL AND EASY REALIZE WHAT HAS HAPPENED, THEIR MOUNTS HAVE COLLAPSED, WITH THEIR THROATS CUT.
HI-YI! EVERY MAN FOR HIMSELF.
IMMEDIATELY, THE DONKEY MEN SCATTER TO THE FOUR WINDS, LEAVING EASY BEWILDERED AS TO WHICH ONE TO CHASE.

May 1934

EASY OVERTAKES A DRIVER, BEATS HIM UP, AND DUMPS THE CHESTS ON THE GROUND.
THEN, MOUNTING THE DONKEY, HE STARTS IN PURSUIT OF ANOTHER DRIVER.
BUT, EVERY TIME HE UNLOADS SOME CHESTS AND STARTS IN PURSUIT OF ANOTHER DONKEY, WATCHFUL DRIVERS DASH UP AND RUN AWAY WITH THE VERY CHESTS HE HAS UNLOADED.
ALL TOLD, EASY RECOVERS ONLY TWO CHESTS.
ROY CRANE © 1934
ROSE PETAL IS HEARTBROKEN.
O MASTER, YOU HAVE BEEN STRIPPED OF YOUR RICHES--- THE EVIL ROGUES WERE TOO CLEVER FOR YOU.
THEY WERE, EH? WELL, JUST TAKE A LOOK AT THOSE CHESTS.
THIS UNCOMPREHENDING PERSON GAZES AT AN UGLY, WORTHLESS COLLECTION OF ROCKS.
SURE! I HAD AN IDEA THOSE MUGS WOULD TRY TO PULL A FAST ONE, SO I BURIED THE GOLD LAST NIGHT, AND REFILLED THE CHESTS WITH ROCKS.
5-6
NEXT WEEK: HOME COMING
CAPTAIN EASY BY ROY CRANE

CAPTAIN EASY
SOLDIER OF FORTUNE
by ROY CRANE
DESERTED BY THEIR DONKEY DRIVERS, EASY AND ROSE PETAL START ACROSS THE DESERT AFOOT. THEY HAVE NEITHER FOOD NOR WATER, AND ROSE PETAL'S FEET ARE SOON BLEEDING FROM THE THORNS.
I'LL CARRY YOU.
I WONDER, SUH, IF YOU'LL SELL US SOME BREAD AND CHEESE.
?
AT LAST THEY COME TO A WATER HOLE, WHERE SITS A LONE TRAVELER, EATING HIS NOON-DAY MEAL.
GLORY BE! AIN'T YOU AN AMERICAN? PUT 'ER THERE, PAL. SO AM I!
RAMBLIN' JACK. THA'S ME. BIN ALL OVER. DONE EVERYTHING. DOGGONE, BUT I'M GLAD TO SEE YA, PAL. THOUGHT I WUZ THE ONLY WHITE MAN IN 500 MILES. HERE, HELP YASELF.
HOW THE BLAZES DID YOU GET HERE, FLY?
NOT ME. KNOW A SECRET PASS THRU THE HIMALAYAS. HERE, HAVE A CIGAR, BUDDIE - TRY THESE PEACHES.
THANKS. IF YOU DON'T MIND, I'LL TAKE A BOWL TO THE GIRL.
THE GIRL? WELL, DOGGONE MY HIDE! WHERE'D YA PICK UP A BEAUT LIKE THAT?

157

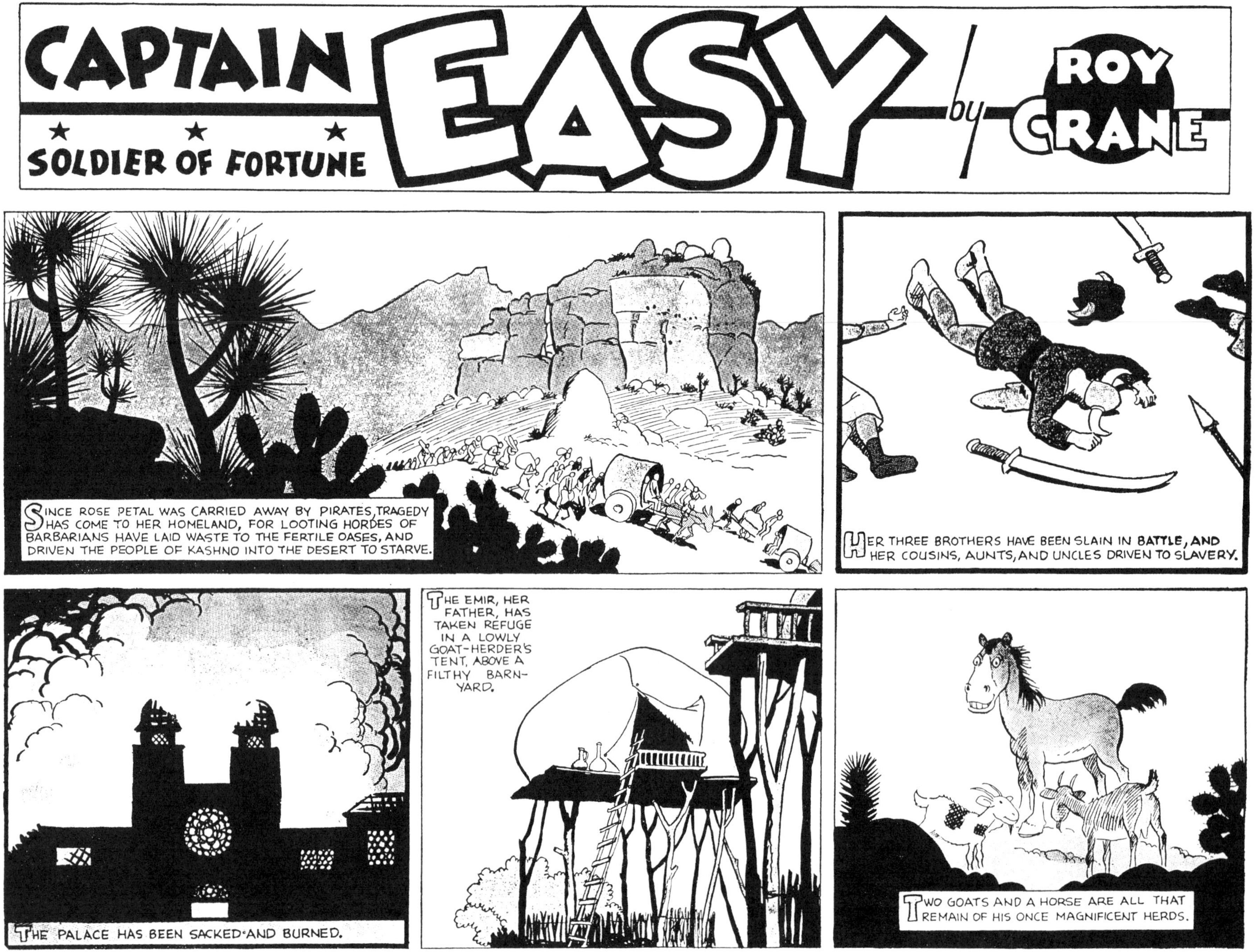
CAPTAIN EASY
SOLDIER OF FORTUNE
by ROY CRANE
SINCE ROSE PETAL WAS CARRIED AWAY BY PIRATES, TRAGEDY HAS COME TO HER HOMELAND, FOR LOOTING HORDES OF BARBARIANS HAVE LAID WASTE TO THE FERTILE OASES, AND DRIVEN THE PEOPLE OF KASHNO INTO THE DESERT TO STARVE.
HER THREE BROTHERS HAVE BEEN SLAIN IN BATTLE, AND HER COUSINS, AUNTS, AND UNCLES DRIVEN TO SLAVERY.
THE PALACE HAS BEEN SACKED AND BURNED.
THE EMIR, HER FATHER, HAS TAKEN REFUGE IN A LOWLY GOAT-HERDER'S TENT, ABOVE A FILTHY BARN-YARD.
TWO GOATS AND A HORSE ARE ALL THAT REMAIN OF HIS ONCE MAGNIFICENT HERDS.

159

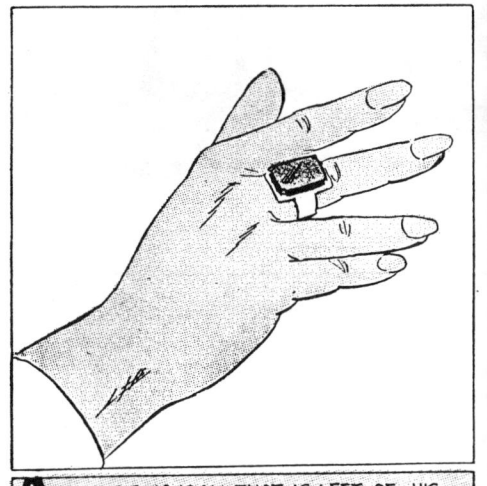

CAPTAIN EASY
SOLDIER OF FORTUNE
by ROY CRANE
AT THE FIRST OPPORTUNITY, RAMBLING JACK SLIPS AWAY FROM EASY, AND HURRIES TO THE EMIR.
BOY! HERE'S MY CHANCE TO CLEAN UP.
HEY, BUDDIE, STEP IN OUTA THE LIGHT. LOOK!
!
LIVING IN A PRIMITIVE WORLD, CUT OFF FROM CIVILIZATION, THE EMIR IS DUMBFOUNDED AT THE SIGHT OF A SIMPLE FLASHLIGHT.
THE CURIOUS OBJECT OF THE SUN PLEASES ME. I WOULD GLADLY GIVE MY TWO WELL-FED GOATS FOR IT.
HO-HO-HO! I GUESS YA WOULD—AND A THOUSAN' MORE TO BOOT, IF YA HAD'EM.
THA'S WHITE MAN'S MAGIC. BUT YOU AIN'T SEEN NOTHIN' YET. LISTEN TO THIS. LISTEN!
TAH-RAH-RAH-RAH BOOM-TEE-AY!
BY THE PINK BEARD OF THE PROPHET! A MIRACLE! A MIRACLE!
IN A FEW MOMENTS, HALF THE VILLAGERS ARE GATHERED AROUND, JABBERING EXCITEDLY, AND TRYING TO GET CLOSER.
BEHOLD! HE HAS A TINY BOX, IN WHICH LIVE COUNTLESS MUSICIANS.
LET US POUR WINE TO THEM THRU THE LITTLE FUNNEL, TO SHOW OUR APPRECIATION.
HEY, NIX, BOYS! STAND BACK.

161

CAPTAIN EASY
SOLDIER OF FORTUNE
by ROY CRANE
June 1934
STRANGE! THERE WERE HUNDREDS OF DOGS WHEN WE FIRST CAME HERE — NOW THERE'S HARDLY A ONE.
TAKING THE CHIPMUNK HOME FOR A PET, SON?
AS WE HAVE EATEN NOTHING SINCE YESTERDAY MORNING, O NOTED ONE, I AM TAKING THE LOWLY RODENT HOME FOR MY MAMA'S SUPPER.
SUPPER? AND WHAT'S THAT FELLA DOING?
HE IS GUARDING THE ONLY CHICKEN LEFT IN THE VILLAGE, SO THAT NO ONE WILL STEAL AN EGG — IF ONE IS EVER LAID.
EASY HEARS THE TEARFUL PRAYERS FOR FOOD, AT THE ALTAR OF ETERNAL FLAME, AND SUDDENLY REALIZES THAT THE PEOPLE OF KASHNO ARE STARVING....
.....THAT THEY ARE DYING OF HUNGER.

NATURALLY, HE IS DEEPLY TOUCHED WHEN THE EMIR, HONORING HIM, GIVES A FEAST WHICH IS ATTENDED BY RAMBLING JACK AND ALL THE BIG SHOTS OF THE VILLAGE.

ESPECIALLY IS EASY TOUCHED UPON LEARNING THAT THE LAST EGG AND THE ONE AND ONLY CHICKEN WERE SERVED TO HIM, WHILE THE OTHERS ATE SPARINGLY OF BOILED GOAT MEAT.

TO EASY'S WAY OF THINKING, NO GREATER SACRIFICE, NO FINER SHOW OF HOSPITALITY, COULD BE MADE, AND HE LEAVES PROMPTLY FOR THE DESERT, WITH A DOZEN MEN.

THERE, HE UNEARTHS THE HUGE SUM OF GOLD HE SO WISELY BURIED, AND GIVES HALF OF IT TO THE EMIR.

MAY YOUR PEOPLE SUH, GO HUNGRY NO MORE.

O MY SON, YOUR SOUL IS A SWEET-SCENTED BUTTERCUP WHICH BLOSSOMS IN AN ASH-HEAP OF HUMAN UGLINESS. THE CHICKADEES HAVE RETURNED TO OUR SONGLESS HEARTS, THE BOBOLINKS HAVE —

AW, LAY OFF THE BUTTERCUP STUFF.

AND, AS FOR THE CHICKADEES, SUH, THE BLASTED DONKEY MEN, WHO CAME SO NEAR STEALING THIS GOLD ONCE BEFORE, ARE HIDING JUST BEYOND THAT HILL. THEY'RE WATCHING EVERY MOVE WE MAKE.

!

NEXT WEEK: WELLS OF PLENTY

CAPTAIN EASY by ROY CRANE
SOLDIER OF FORTUNE

QUIETLY, FOR ALL ARE ASLEEP.
IN ONE WELL, THEY HIDE THE GOLD WHICH IS TO BUY FOOD FOR STARVING REFUGEES OF KASHNO
IN ANOTHER WELL, THEY DROP THE GOLD WHICH IS TO REMAIN EASY'S SHARE.
THERE, O MERCIFUL BENEFACTOR. IT WILL BE SAFE FROM PRYING EYES, UNDER TEN FEET OF WATER.
BUT ARE THESE BOZOS TO BE TRUSTED?
WHEN ONE IS SWORN TO SECRECY, BEFORE THE ALTAR OF 10,000 HONORED ANCESTORS, O DUBIOUS ONE, NO POWER ON EARTH COULD UNSEAL HIS DETERMINED LIPS.
TWELVE MEN, ONE BY ONE, KNEEL BEFORE THE TOWERING, STONE IMAGE AND SOLEMNLY SLASH THEIR CHESTS UNTIL COVERED WITH BLOOD.
HEAR ME, O WORSHIPFUL ANCESTORS! HEAR ME! MAY THIS PERSON BE TORTURED UNTIL DEAD. MAY HIS SOUL BE CAST INTO EVERLASTING FIRE, MAY HIS DESCENDANTS, UNTO THE HUNDREDTH GENERATION, SUFFER UNMENTIONABLE SHAME AND DISGRACE, BEFORE A SECRET, LEARNED BY ME THIS NIGHT, IS BETRAYED.
CAPTAIN EASY
SOLDIER OF FORTUNE

165

CAPTAIN EASY
SOLDIER OF FORTUNE
by ROY CRANE
BLESSINGS OF THE SEVEN HEAVENS UPON YOU, O WONDROUS ONE.
SENSING THAT THE UNEXPECTED APPEARANCE OF GOATS, CHICKENS, HOGS AND GRAIN IN THEIR STARVING MIDST, IS DUE TO EASY, THE PEOPLE OF KASHNO ALL BUT WORSHIP THAT SILENT-SPOKEN INDIVIDUAL.
RAMBLING JACK GIVES A KNOWING GRUNT, FOR HE HAS SECRETLY DISCOVERED THE HIDDEN STORE OF GOLD.
HE BECOMES UNBEARABLY CHESTY.
MAKE WAY FER A BIG SHOT, YOU SPRADDLE-LEGGED PEANUT!
AND BEHAVES LIKE A MANIAC.
HO HO! I'M A RIP-SNORTIN' BUCKO, GIRLIE, AND THE BEST AIN'T NONE TOO GOOD FER ME.
!

CAPTAIN EASY BY ROY CRANE

CAPTAIN EASY
SOLDIER OF FORTUNE
by ROY CRANE
NOW GET THE BLAZES OUT O' CAMP AS FAST AS YOU CAN TRAVEL!
YOU BET I WILL!
YOU BET! AND WHEN I GIT BACK, MISTER, YOU'LL KNOW IT!
AS HIS RASCALLY COUNTRYMAN PACKS AND DEPARTS, EASY HEAVES A SIGH OF RELIEF.
BUT THE EMIR CONSULTS WITH HIS SPIES AND IS ALARMED.
EH? HE HAS BEEN SEEN LOITERING ABOUT THE DRINKING WELLS.
AIE, O PEERLESS GEM OF WISDOM. IT IS SUSPECTED THAT HE KNOWS THEIR PRICELESS CONTENTS.
THEN FOLLOW HIM, KABOOLA! FOLLOW HIM, AND SEE THAT HIS TREACHEROUS TONGUE IS SILENCED.
AT THE SIGHT OF ARMED HORSEMEN DASHING AFTER HIM, RAMBLING JACK'S BLOOD RUNS COLD, AND HE BEATS HIS CAMELS TO A GALLOP.

BUT, BEFORE THEY CAN OVERTAKE HIS CLUMSY STEEDS, A THOUSAND GRINNING, HALF-CLAD SAVAGES APPEAR UNEXPECTEDLY FROM BEHIND A HILL.
THE KASHNO WARRIORS TURN AND FLEE BACK TO THEIR VILLAGE.
THE SAVAGE CHIEFTAIN ROARS AT JACK.
HOLD! I AM GHARBISH KHAN, MIGHTY DESTROYER OF DEVIL-DEMONS, AND CONQUEROR OF KASHNO. WHY FLEE YOU FROM MY DESPISED ENEMIES?
IT'S HEALTHY, THA'S WHY! I KNOW TOO MUCH.
AH, INDEED? INCREDIBLE TALES REACH MY EARS THAT CERTAIN DONKEY DRIVERS HAVE SEEN THE EMIR UNEARTH VAST SUMS OF HIDDEN GOLD.
IN GRATITUDE FOR SAVING YOUR LIFE, O HUMOROUSLY DRESSED ONE, MAYHAP YOU WILL INFORM THIS EAGER PERSON AS TO THE TRUTH.
I KIN DO BETTER THAN THAT. LISSEN, SPORT, GIMME A 50-50 SPLIT AND I'LL SHOW YOU WHERE IT'S HID.
NEXT WEEK: THE BETRAYER.
CAPTAIN EASY
SOLDIER OF FORTUNE
by ROY CRANE

CAPTAIN EASY
SOLDIER OF FORTUNE
by ROY CRANE
July 1934
IT IS AGREED, O BROTHER.
ATTABOY! YOU RUN 'EM OUT, AND WE'LL SPLIT THE BLOOMING BOOTY.
AFTER LISTENING TO RAMBLING JACK'S LURID ACCOUNT OF THE VAST RICHES HIDDEN IN THE KASHNO VILLAGE, GARBISH KHAN DETERMINES TO CRUSH THE HATED EMIR ONCE AND FOR ALL.
MEANWHILE, THE ALARMED VILLAGERS HERD THEIR CATTLE AND GOATS INTO PENS.
HI YI! UP WITH THE LADDER.
AND TAKE REFUGE IN THEIR QUEER LITTLE TENTS ON STILTS.
THEIR PLIGHT SEEMS HOPELESS.
WE ARE OUTNUMBERED TEN TO ONE.
WELL, WHAT THE BLAZES! A FELLA HAS TO DIE SOONER OR LATER. LET 'EM COME.
THE BARBARIANS CHARGE THRU THE VILLAGE LIKE A THUNDERING AVALANCHE.

CAPTAIN EASY by ROY CRANE

CAPTAIN EASY
SOLDIER OF FORTUNE
by ROY CRANE
HA YA! IT IS A HEAVEN-SENT MESSAGE FROM THE GODS.
GARBISH KHAN, MIGHTY BARBARIAN CHIEFTAIN, CASTS AN APPROVING EYE AT HIS FOLLOWERS TRYING TO SHIELD THEIR CAMPFIRES FROM A RAPIDLY RISING WIND.......
.... AND COMMANDS HIS MEN TO BUILD A WALL OF DRIED BRUSH 20 FEET HIGH ON THE WINDWARD SIDE OF THE KASHNO VILLAGE.
THEN, FORMING HIS WARRIORS AROUND THE VILLAGE, HE SETS FIRE TO THE BRUSH.
INSTANTLY THE INFLAMMABLE MASS BECOMES A RAGING INFERNO.

CAPTAIN EASY BY ROY CRANE

Panel 1: Billowing clouds of smoke envelope the village.

Panel 2: Flames leap quickly to the flimsy tents.

Panel 3: The heat and smoke become unbearable. Pigs squeal in terror. Cattle and goats are burned alive. The wretched people of Kashno stagger into the desert, driven out of their homes for the second time by their cruel and relentless enemy.

Panel 4: Meanwhile, Rambling Jack, the betrayer, sights an alluring figure stumbling blindly thru the smoke.
— "Well, bus' my neck if'n it aint Rose Petal!"

Panel 5: "Giddup, ya old son of inequity. Here's where I captures myself a prisoner of war."

Panel 6:
— "Who's there? I am lost. I cannot see."
— "Quick, gal! Gimme yer hand. Me 'n' Easy's made up. He's bin runnin' wild lookin' fer ya, an' says for me to bring ya to 'im."

NEXT WEEK: THE PRISONER

© 1934 BY NEA SERVICE, INC.

173

Panel 1:

"O FOUL BETRAYER! O BROTHER OF A CAMEL'S BREATH! RELEASE ME."

TOO LATE, ROSE PETAL REALIZES THAT RAMBLING JACK HAS LIED TO HER, THAT HE HAS NO INTENTION OF RETURNING HER TO HER PEOPLE, AS HE PROMISED.

Panel 2:

INSTEAD, SHE IS DRAGGED INTO THE ROWDY CAMP OF THE UNSPEAKABLE BARBARIANS.

"HA YAH! THE PALPITATING HEART OF THIS HE-PERSON IS THRILLED BY THE SIGHT OF ONE SO DEMURE AND GRACEFUL."

"HEY, YOU! SHE'S MY PRISONER OF WAR, GET ME! MINE! MINE!!"

Panel 3:

THE EYES OF GHARBISH KHAN GLITTER WITH HATRED, BUT HIS VOICE HAS THE SMOOTHNESS OF SATIN.

"FOR THE MOMENT, O INVALUABLE ONE, GOLD IS MORE PRECIOUS THAN WILLOWY WENCHES. PRAY SHOW ME THE HIDDEN RICHES OF KASHNO."

Panel 4:

"THERE! IN THE WELLS."

"FAH! A CHILD WOULD HAVE GUESSED IT. WHAT A FOOL WAS I, WHEN I AGREED TO SHARE WITH YOU A FORTUNE SO EASILY FOUND."

174

175

176

177

CAPTAIN EASY, SUH, CHINESE AIR CORPS.
LIEUTENANT HUNTER, SIR, BRITISH ROYAL AIR FORCE, KIKOPAL, INDIA. I SAY, OLD CHAP, I'M JOLLY WELL WASHED OUT— SICK. IS THERE A TELEGRAPH HANDY?
A TELEGRAPH! WHERE THE BLINKING BLAZES YOU THINK YOU ARE?
REALLY, OLD BOY, I—I'M IN A BIT OF A FOG. ACUTE APPENDICITIS. AFRAID I CAN'T CARRY ON. LOST MY BEARINGS YESTERDAY— FORCED LANDING — PETROL SUPPLY NEARLY EXHAUSTED.
© 1934
7-22
JOLLY PREDICAMENT, EH, WHAT?
JOLLY? MAN, IT'S A PICNIC. YOU'VE NO MACHINE GUN, AND YOU'RE JUST IN TIME TO BE ATTACKED BY A THOUSAND SAVAGES.
NEXT WEEK:
THE DEVIL'S BREATH
CAPTAIN EASY
SOLDIER OF FORTUNE
EH? WE'RE ABOUT TO BE ATTACKED BY A THOUSAND SAVAGES?
EXACTLY! AND YOU HAVEN'T A MACHINE GUN ON YOUR PLANE. I TELL YOU, FELLA, WE'RE IN A HOLE. WE GOT TO THINK FAST. HAVEN'T YOU ANY BOMBS, OR GRENADES?
I'M SO BEASTLY ILL, I— OH, I SAY! THERE'S A SMOKE-SCREEN DEVICE. WOULD THAT HELP?
GREAT! WHY, MAN, ANYTHING'S WORTH TRYING.
HI, THERE! GET AWAY! WHAT ARE YOU DOING TO THAT SHIP?
SH-H! WE ARE GOING TO SLAY THE FIERCE DEVIL-MONSTER WHILE IT SLEEPS, O, HONORED ONE.

LIKE BLAZES YOU ARE! HERE— DRAW ME THE SYMBOL OF THE DRAGON OF DEATH.
AIE. IT IS A CIRCLE, LIKE THIS, WITH A TAIL.
A CIRCLE WITH A TAIL— THAT'S A CINCH.
EASY LEAPS INTO THE COCK-PIT, AND RAPIDLY CLIMBS TO A HEIGHT OF TWO MILES. FAR BELOW, THE BARBARIANS ARE MASSING FOR AN ATTACK.
THERE IS NO TIME TO LOSE. EASY SWINGS IN A WIDE CIRCLE, LEAVING A DENSE CLOUD OF SMOKE IN HIS WAKE.
AND ADDS A TAIL.
SEEING THE CLOUD-LIKE SYMBOL OF THE DRAGON OF DEATH, THE SUPERSTITIOUS NATIVES TREMBLE WITH FEAR.
LOOK! LOOK! IT IS A WARNING FROM THE GODS OF THE UPPER AIR.
AH YEE! WE HAVE DISPLEASED THE HEAVENLY SPIRITS WITH OUR CONQUESTS.

180

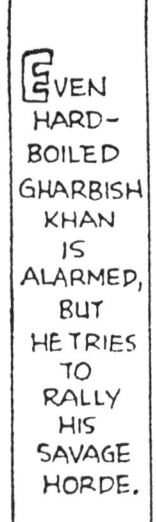

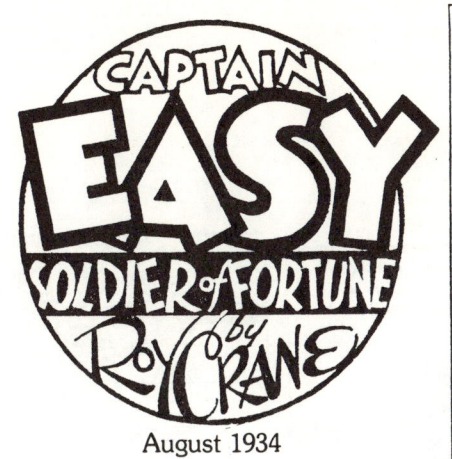

CAPTAIN EASY
SOLDIER of FORTUNE
by Roy Crane

August 1934

No wonder that the barbarians are terrified when Easy does a power dive at them.

For they have never heard of airplanes. They are savages who believe that the clouds and stars are homes of evil spirits.

181

They believe that the end of all things will come when a fierce devil-monster descends from the upper air to devour the world.

And they believe that Easy's plane is that very devil monster, coming to destroy them.

"Eeyi! It is the end of all earthly existence."

Suddenly, however, the plane begins to sputter.

"Wup! Outa gas."

FFT! FFT!

183

DISHEARTENED, EASY WATCHES 13 DEVIL-DOCTORS GATHER AROUND THE ENGLISHMAN. SOLEMNLY, THEY BOW THREE TIMES, AND EACH LEAVES HIS SECRET CURE-ALL.

"BAH! RATS! HOW YOU GOING TO KNOW WHICH MEDICINE TO GIVE HIM? YOU CAN'T EXPECT HIM TO DRINK ALL 13."

"AIE! WE SHALL SUMMON THE WITCH-WOMAN TO SELECT THE RIGHT JAR."

WHILE A DAUGHTER BLOWS LUSTILY ON A DEVIL-HORN, MAMA WITCH MUMBLES MAGIC WORDS OVER THE JARS OF MEDICINE. AT LAST, SHE SELECTS ONE AS BEING HEAVEN-SENT.

THIS, SHE GIVES TO THE ENGLISHMAN, AND HANGS THE OTHER TWELVE JARS HIGH IN THE TREES.

CAPTAIN EASY by ROY CRANE

CAPTAIN EASY
SOLDIER OF FORTUNE
by ROY CRANE
WHAT'S THAT?
BRUSH, FOR A SIGNAL FIRE. I HAVE A NOTION, OLD CHAP, THAT MY OUTFIT WILL SEND SEARCHING PARTIES.
BLAZES! I - I HOPE SO. I BEEN MAROONED IN THIS BLASTED HOLE FOR MONTHS. IT'S PRACTICALLY IMPOSSIBLE TO GET OUT. MOUNTAINS FOUR MILES HIGH. NO WHITE PEOPLE. NO TRAINS. NO AUTOS. SOMETIMES I THINK I'LL GO NUTTY!
HURRIEDLY, EASY AND LIEUTENANT HUNTER SET FIRE TO THEIR BRUSH PILES, THEN SMOTHER THEM WITH WET GRASS, AND SEND LAZY PUFFS OF SMOKE INTO THE AIR.
SURE ENOUGH, WITHIN THREE DAYS, THE DRONE OF BRITISH PLANES IS HEARD FAR TO THE SOUTH.

187

188

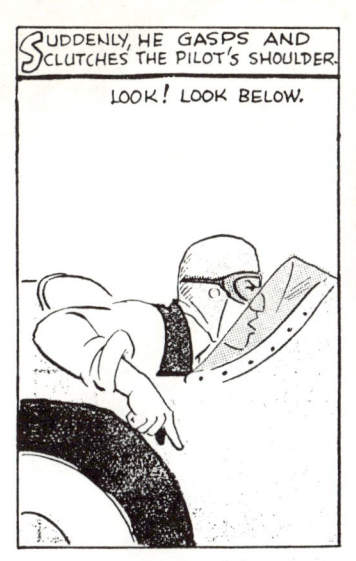

> Suddenly, he gasps and clutches the pilot's shoulder.
>
> LOOK! LOOK BELOW.

> The pilot, too, is startled, and at a signal from him, the four planes drop to a thousand feet.

> There, below them, is a city, apparently deserted, its streets choked with weeds and trees, and its open doorways laced with vines and creepers.

> But most amazing of all, three-fourths of the city is buried beneath the surface of a crystal-clear lake or sea.

FISH SWIM LAZILY IN AND OUT OF WINDOWS, AND LOBSTERS CRAWL OVER COBBLE STONES THAT ONCE KNEW THE TREAD OF HUMAN FEET. ONLY THE TALLEST TOWERS RISE ABOVE THE SURFACE.
© 1934
AFTER CIRCLING LOW SEVERAL TIMES, THE FLYERS TURN AGAIN TOWARD INDIA, FOR THE SURROUNDING REGION IS FAR TOO WILD AND RUGGED TO PERMIT A SAFE LANDING.
CAPTAIN EASY
SOLDIER OF FORTUNE
8-26
PRESENTLY THEY ARE BATTLING THE TREACHEROUS AIR CURRENTS OVER THE GIGANTIC HIMALAYAS, BUT EASY IS UNAWARE OF THE ALTITUDE, AND THE BITTER COLD. HE HAS FORGOTTEN ROSE PETAL AND INDIA — HE IS THINKING OF THE FORGOTTEN CITY.
NEXT WEEK: WHERE EAST MEETS WEST.

TERRY and the Pirates
by Milton Caniff

COLLECTOR'S EDITION
The complete reprint. Each volume 11 x 7½, jacketed, gold stamped, numbered, 320 pages:
Vol. 1-6: sold out

THE WAR YEARS 1940-1946
Vols. 7-12 OF THE GREAT HARDCOVER EDITION AT ALMOST HALF PRICE!
$19.95!

Vol. 7: 1940-1941
Vol. 8: 1941-1942
Vol. 9: sold out
Vol. 10: 1943-1944
Vol. 11: 1944-1945
Vol. 12: 1945-1946

PAPERBACK EDITION
Going over all of Terry & The Pirates by Caniff once again in an affordable format! Each volume is 64 pp., 8½ x 11, color cover. The first volumes covering up to 1940 are out and a new one is issued every 3 months.
Vols. 1-5: $5.95 each; vol. past #5: $6.95 each
Special Offer:
Vols. 1-4 slipcased: $25
Vols. 5-8 slipcased: $25
SUBSCRIBE!
Get any 4 volumes past or future: $25, free P&H!

WE HAVE HUNDREDS OF VERY SATISFIED SUBSCRIBERS!

MISSING ANY VOLUMES?

FLYING BUTTRESS CLASSICS LIBRARY

Bill Blackbeard
Series Editor

The Complete 1924-1943
WASH TUBBS
AND CAPTAIN EASY
by Roy Crane

Each volume of this quarterly 18 volume reprint contains 192 pages of action of this classic which inspired so many adventure strips to come. Available in either a handsome jacketed gold stamped hardcover, or paperback. In a handy 11 x 8½ format with 3 strips per page.
Hardcovers: $32.50 each
Paperbacks: $16.95 each
ALL VOLUMES IN STOCK

SUBSCRIBE!
Only $80 for any 4 hardcovers ($130 separately)
Only $50 for any 4 paperbacks ($67.80 separately)

NBM
35-53 70th St.
Jackson Heights, NY 11372